DR. HEIDENHOFF'S PROCESS

Edward Bellamy

ISBN-13: 978-0-9794154-4-9

TARK
Classic Fiction
2007

P. O. Box 10339
Rockville, MD 20849-0339
United States of America

Contents

CHAPTER I   5

CHAPTER II   19

CHAPTER III   22

CHAPTER IV   36

CHAPTER V   41

CHAPTER VI   51

CHAPTER VII   59

CHAPTER VIII   63

CHAPTER IX   70

CHAPTER X   78

CHAPTER XI   87

CHAPTER XII   98

CHAPTER I

The hand of the clock fastened up on the white wall of the conference room, just over the framed card bearing the words "Stand up for Jesus," and between two other similar cards, respectively bearing the sentences "Come unto Me," and "The Wonderful, the Counsellor," pointed to ten minutes of nine. As was usual at this period of Newville prayer-meetings, a prolonged pause had supervened. The regular standbyes had all taken their usual part, and for any one to speak or pray would have been about as irregular as for one of the regulars to fail in doing so. For the attendants at Newville prayer-meetings were strictly divided into the two classes of speakers and listeners, and, except during revivals or times of special interest, the distinction was scrupulously observed.

Deacon Tuttle had spoken and prayed, Deacon Miller had prayed and spoken, Brother Hunt had amplified a point in last Sunday's sermon, Brother Taylor had called attention to a recent death in the village as a warning to sinners, and Sister Morris had prayed twice, the second time it must be admitted, with a certain perceptible petulance of tone, as if willing to have it understood that she was doing more than ought to be expected of her. But while it was extremely improbable that any others of the twenty or thirty persons assembled would feel called on to break the silence, though it stretched to the crack of doom, yet, on the other hand, to close the meeting before the mill bell had struck nine would have been regarded as a dangerous innovation. Accordingly, it only remained to wait in decorous silence during the remaining ten minutes.

The clock ticked on with that judicial intonation characteristic of time-pieces that measure sacred time and wasted opportunities. At intervals the pastor, with an innocent affectation of having just observed the silence, would remark: "There is yet opportunity. . . . . Time is passing, brethren. . . . . Any brother or sister. . . . . We shall be glad to hear from any one." Farmer Bragg, tired with his day's hoeing, snored quietly in the corner of a seat. Mrs. Parker dropped a hymn-book. Little Tommy Blake, who had fallen over while napping and hit his nose, snivelled under his breath. Madeline Brand, as she sat at the melodeon below the minister's desk, stifled a small yawn with her pretty fingers. A June bug boomed through the open window and circled around Deacon Tuttle's head, affecting that good man with the solicitude characteristic of bald-headed persons when buzzing things are about. Next it made a dive at Madeline, attracted, perhaps, by her shining eyes, and the little gesture of panic with which she evaded it was the prettiest thing in the world; at least, so it seemed to Henry Burr, a broad-shouldered young fellow on the back seat, whose strong, serious face is just now lit up by a pleasant smile.

Mr. Lewis, the minister, being seated directly under the clock, cannot see it without turning around, wherein the audience has an advantage of him, which it makes full use of. Indeed, so closely is the general attention concentrated upon the time-piece, that a stranger might draw the mistaken inference that this was the object for whose worship the little company had gathered. Finally, making a slight concession of etiquette to curiosity, Mr. Lewis turns and looks up at the clock, and, again facing the people, observes, with the air of communicating a piece of intelligence, "There are yet a few moments."

In fact, and not to put too fine a point upon it, there are five minutes left, and the young men on the back seats, who attend prayer-meetings to go home with the girls, are experiencing increasing qualms of alternate hope and fear as the moment draws near when they shall put their fortune to the test, and win or lose it all. As they furtively glance over at the girls, how formidable they look, how superior to common affections, how serenely and icily indifferent, as if the existence of youth of the other sex in their vicinity at that moment was the thought furthest from their minds! How presumptuous, how audacious, to those youth themselves now appears the design, a little while ago so jauntily entertained, of accompanying these dainty beings home, how weak and inadequate the phrases of request which they had framed wherewith to accost them! Madeline Brand is looking particularly grave, as becomes a young lady who knows that she has three would-be escorts waiting for her just outside the church door, not to count one or two within, between whose conflicting claims she has only five minutes more to make up her mind.

The minister had taken up his hymn-book, and was turning over the leaves to select the closing hymn, when some one rose in the back part of the room. Every head turned as if pulled by one wire to see who it was, and Deacon Tuttle put on his spectacles to inspect more closely this dilatory person, who was moved to exhortation at so unnecessary a time.

It was George Bayley, a young man of good education, excellent training, and once of great promise, but of most unfortunate recent experience. About a year previous he had embezzled a small amount of the funds of a corporation in Newville, of which he was paymaster, for the purpose of raising money for a pressing emergency. Various circumstances

7

showed that his repentance had been poignant, even before his theft was discovered. He had reimbursed the corporation, and there was no prosecution, because his dishonest act had been no part of generally vicious habits, but a single unaccountable deflection from rectitude. The evident intensity of his remorse had excited general sympathy, and when Parker, the village druggist, gave him employment as clerk, the act was generally applauded, and all the village folk had endeavoured with one accord, by a friendly and hearty manner, to make him feel that they were disposed to forget the past, and help him to begin life over again. He had been converted at a revival the previous winter, but was counted to have backslidden of late, and become indifferent to religion. He looked badly. His face was exceedingly pale, and his eyes were sunken. But these symptoms of mental sickness were dominated by an expression of singular peace and profound calm. He had the look of one whom, after a wasting illness, the fever has finally left; of one who has struggled hard, but whose struggle is over. And his voice, when he began to speak, was very soft and clear.

"If it will not be too great an inconvenience," he said; "I should like to keep you a few minutes while I talk about myself a little. You remember, perhaps, that I professed to be converted last winter. Since then I am aware that I have shown a lack of interest in religious matters, which has certainly justified you in supposing that I was either hasty or insincere in my profession. I have made my arrangements to leave you soon, and should be sorry to have that impression remain on the minds of my friends. Hasty I may have been, but not insincere. Perhaps you will excuse me if I refer to an unpleasant subject, but I can make my meaning clearer by reviewing a little of my unfortunate history."

The suavity with which he apologized for alluding to his own ruin, as if he had passed beyond the point of any personal feeling in the matter, had something uncanny and creeping in its effect on the listeners, as if they heard a dead soul speaking through living lips.

"After my disgrace," pursued the young man in the same quietly explanatory tone, "the way I felt about myself was very much, I presume, as a mechanic feels, who by an unlucky stroke has hopelessly spoiled the looks of a piece of work, which he nevertheless has got to go on and complete as best he can. Now you know that in order to find any pleasure in his work, the workman must be able to take a certain amount of pride in it. Nothing is more disheartening for him than to have to keep on with a job with which he must be disgusted every time he returns to it, every time his eye glances it over. Do I make my meaning clear? I felt like that beaten crew in last week's regatta, which, when it saw itself hopelessly distanced at the very outset, had no pluck to row out the race, but just pulled ashore and went home.

"Why, I remember when I was a little boy in school, and one day made a big blot on the very first page of my new copybook, that I didn't have the heart to go on any further, and I recollect well how I teased my father to buy me a new book, and cried and sulked until he finally took his knife and neatly cut out the blotted page. Then I was comforted and took heart, and I believe I finished that copybook so well that the teacher gave me the prize.

"Now you see, don't you," he continued, the ghost of a smile glimmering about his eyes, "how it was that after my disgrace I couldn't seem to take an interest any more in anything? Then came the revival, and that gave me a notion that religion might help me. I had heard, from a child, that the blood of Christ had a power to wash away sins and to leave one white and spotless with a sense of being new and clean every whit. That was what I wanted, just what I wanted. I am sure that you never had a more sincere, more dead-in-earnest convert than I was."

He paused a moment, as if in mental contemplation, and then the words dropped slowly from his lips, as a dim self-pitying smile rested on his haggard face.

"I really think you would be sorry for me if you knew how very bitter was my disappointment when I found that, these bright promises were only figurative expressions which I had taken literally. Doubtless I should not have fallen into such a ridiculous mistake if my great need had not made my wishes fathers to my thoughts. Nobody was at all to blame but myself; nobody at all. I'm blaming no one. Forgiving sins, I should have known, is not blotting, them out. The blood of Christ only turns them red instead of black. It leaves them in the record. It leaves them in the memory. That day when I blotted my copybook at school, to have had the teacher forgive me ever so kindly would not have made me feel the least bit better so long as the blot was there. It wasn't any penalty from without, but the hurt to my own pride which the spot made, that I wanted taken away, so I might get heart to go on. Supposing one of you—and you'll excuse me for asking you to put yourself a moment in my place—had picked a pocket. Would it make a great deal of difference in your state of mind that the person whose pocket you had picked kindly forgave you, and declined to prosecute? Your offence against him was trifling, and easily repaired. Your chief offence was against yourself, and that was irreparable. No other person with his forgiveness can mediate between you and yourself. Until you have been in such a fix, you can't imagine, perhaps, how curiously impertinent it sounds to hear talk about somebody else forgiving you for ruining yourself. It is like mocking."

The nine o'clock bell pealed out from the mill tower.

"I am trespassing on your kindness, but I have only a few more words to say. The ancients had a beautiful fable about the water of Lethe, in which the soul that was bathed straightway forgot all that was sad and evil in its previous life; the most stained, disgraced, and mournful of souls coming

10

forth fresh, blithe, and bright as a baby's. I suppose my absurd misunderstanding arose from a vague notion that the blood of Christ had in it something like this virtue of Lethe water. Just think how blessed a thing for men it would be if such were indeed the case, if their memories could be cleansed and disinfected at the same time their hearts were purified! Then the most disgraced and ashamed might live good and happy lives again. Men would be redeemed from their sins in fact, and not merely in name. The figurative promises of the Gospel would become literally true. But this is idle dreaming. I will not keep you," and, checking himself abruptly, he sat down.

The moment he did so, Mr. Lewis rose and pronounced the benediction, dismissing the meeting without the usual closing hymn. He was afraid that something might be said by Deacon Tuttle or Deacon Miller, who were good men, but not very subtle in their spiritual insight, which would still further alienate the unfortunate young man. His own intention of finding opportunity for a little private talk with him after the meeting was, however, disappointed by the promptness with which Bayley left the room. He did not seem to notice the sympathetic faces and out-stretched hands around him. There was a set smile on his face, and his eyes seemed to look through people without seeing them. There was a buzz of conversation as the people began to talk together of the decided novelty in the line of conference-meeting exhortations to which they had just listened. The tone of almost all was sympathetic, though many were shocked and pained, and others declared that they did not understand what he had meant. Many insisted that he must be a little out of his head, calling attention to the fact that he looked so pale. None of these good hearts were half so much offended by anything heretical in the utterances of the young man as they were stirred with sympathy for his evident discouragement. Mr. Lewis was perhaps the only one who had received a very distinct impression of the line of thought underlying his words, and he came walking down the aisle with his head bent and a very grave face, not joining any of the groups which were engaged in talk. Henry Burr was standing near the door, his hat in his hand, watching Madeline out of the corners of his eyes, as she closed the melodeon and adjusted her shawl.

"Good-evening, Henry," said Mr. Lewis, pausing beside the young man. "Do you know whether anything unpleasant has happened to George lately to account for what he said to-night?"

"I do not, sir," replied Henry.

"I had a fancy that he might have been slighted by some one, or given the cold shoulder. He is very sensitive."

"I don't think any one in the village would slight him," said Henry.

"I should have said so too," remarked the minister, reflectively. "Poor boy, poor boy! He seems to feel very badly, and it is hard to know how to cheer him."

"Yes, sir—that is—certainly," replied Henry incoherently, for Madeline was now coming down the aisle.

In his own preoccupation not noticing the young man's, Mr. Lewis passed out.

As she approached the door Madeline was talking animatedly with another young lady.

"Good-evening," said Henry.

"Poor fellow!" continued Madeline to her companion, "he seemed quite hopeless."

"Good-evening," repeated Henry.

Looking around, she appeared to observe him for the first time. "Good-evening," she said.

"May I escort you home?" he asked, becoming slightly red in the face.

She looked at him for a moment as if she could scarcely believe her ears that such an audacious proposal had been made to her. Then she said, with a bewitching smile—

"I shall be much obliged."

As he drew her arm beneath his own the contact diffused an ecstatic sensation of security through his stalwart but tremulous limbs. He had got her, and his tribulations were forgotten. For a while they walked silently along the dark streets, both too much impressed by the tragic suggestions of poor Bayley's outbreak to drop at once into trivialities. For it must be understood that Madeline's little touch of coquetry had been merely instinctive, a sort of unconscious reflex action of the feminine nervous system, quite consistent with very lugubrious engrossments.

To Henry there was something strangely sweet in sharing with her for the first time a mood of solemnity, seeing that their intercourse had always before been in the vein of pleasantry and badinage common to the first stages of courtships. This new experience appeared to dignify their relation, and weave them together with a new strand. At length she said—

"Why didn't you go after poor George and cheer him up instead of going home with me? Anybody could have done that."

"No doubt," replied Henry, seriously; "but, if I'd left anybody else to do it, I should have needed cheering up as much as George does."

"Dear me," she exclaimed, as a little smile, not exactly of vexation, curved her lips under cover of the darkness, "you take a most unwarrantable liberty in being jealous of me. I never gave you nor anybody else any right to be, and I won't have it!"

"Very well. It shall be just as you say," he replied. The sarcastic humility of his tone made her laugh in spite of herself, and she immediately changed the subject, demanding—

"Where is Laura to-night?"

"She's at home, making cake for the picnic," he said.

"The good girl! and I ought to be making some, too. I wonder if poor George will be at the picnic?"

13

"I doubt it," said Henry. "You know he never goes to any sort of party. The last time I saw him at such a place was at Mr. Bradford's. He was playing whist, and they were joking about cheating. Somebody said—Mr. Bradford it was—'I can trust my wife's honesty. She doesn't know enough to cheat, but I don't know about George.' George was her partner. Bradford didn't mean any harm; he forgot, you see. He'd have bitten his tongue off otherwise sooner than have said it. But everybody saw the application, and there was a dead silence. George got red as fire, and then pale as death. I don't know how they finished the hand, but presently somebody made an excuse, and the game was broken off."

"Oh, dear! dear! That was cruel! cruel! How could Mr. Bradford do it? I should think he would never forgive himself! never!" exclaimed Madeline, with an accent of poignant sympathy, involuntarily pressing Henry's arm, and thereby causing him instantly to forget all about George and his misfortunes, and setting his heart to beating so tumultuously that he was afraid she would notice it and be offended. But she did not seem to be conscious of the intoxicating effluence she was giving forth, and presently added, in a tone of sweetest pity—

"He used to be so frank and dashing in his manner, and now when he meets one of us girls on the street he seems so embarrassed, and looks away or at the ground, as if he thought we should not like to bow to him, or meant to cut him. I'm sure we'd cut our heads off sooner. It's enough to make one cry, such times, to see how wretched he is, and so sensitive that no one can say a word to cheer him. Did you notice what he said about leaving town? I hadn't heard anything about it before, had you?"

"No," said Henry, "not a word. Wonder where he's going. Perhaps he thinks it will be easier for him in some place where they don't know him."

They walked on in silence a few moments, and then Madeline said, in a musing tone—

"How strange it would seem if one really could have unpleasant things blotted out of their memories! What dreadful thing would you forget now, if you could? Confess."

"I would blot out the recollection that you went boat-riding with Will Taylor last Wednesday afternoon, and what I've felt about it ever since."

"Dear me, Mr. Henry Burr," said Madeline, with an air of excessive disdain, "how long is it since I authorized you to concern yourself with my affairs? If it wouldn't please you too much, I'd certainly box your ears.

"I think you're rather unreasonable," he protested, in a hurt tone. "You said a minute ago that you wouldn't permit me to be jealous of you, and just because I'm so anxious to obey you that I want to forget that I ever was, you are vexed."

A small noise, expressive of scorn, and not to be represented by letters of the alphabet, was all the reply she deigned to this more ingenious than ingenuous plea.

"I've made my confession, and it's only fair you should make yours," he said next. "What remorseful deed have you done that you'd like to forget?"

"You needn't speak in that babying tone. I fancy I could commit sins as well as you, with all your big moustache, if I wanted to. I don't believe you'd hurt a fly, although you do look so like a pirate. You've probably got a goody little conscience, so white and soft that you'd die of shame to have people see it."

"Excuse me, Lady Macbeth," he said, laughing; "I don't wish to underrate your powers of depravity, but which of your soul-destroying sins would you prefer to forget, if indeed any of them are shocking enough to trouble your excessively hardened conscience?

"Well, I must admit," said Madeline, seriously, "that I wouldn't care to forget anything I've done, not even my faults and follies. I should be afraid if they were taken away that I shouldn't have any character left."

15

"Don't put it on that ground," said Henry, "it's sheer vanity that makes you say so. You know your faults are just big enough to be beauty-spots, and that's why you'd rather keep 'em."

She reflected a moment, and then said, decisively—

"That's a compliment. I don't believe I like 'em from you. Don't make me any more."

Perhaps she did not take the trouble to analyse the sentiment that prompted her words. Had she done so, she would doubtless have found it in a consciousness when in his presence of being surrounded with so fine and delicate an atmosphere of unspoken devotion that words of flattery sounded almost gross.

They paused before a gate. Pushing it open and passing within, she said, "Good-night."

"One word more. I have a favour to ask," he said. "May I take you to the picnic?"

"Why, I think no escort will be necessary," she replied; "we go in broad daylight; and there are no bears or Indians at Hemlock Hollow."

"But your basket. You'll need somebody to carry your basket."

"Oh yes, to be sure, my basket," she exclaimed, with an ironical accent. "It will weigh at least two pounds, and I couldn't possibly carry it myself, of course. By all means come, and much obliged for your thoughtfulness."

But as she turned to go in she gave him a glance which had just enough sweetness in it to neutralize the irony of her words. In the treatment of her lovers, Madeline always punctured the skin before applying a drop of sweetness, and perhaps this accounted for the potent effect it had to inflame the blood, compared with more profuse but superficial applications of less sharp-tongued maidens.

Henry waited until the graceful figure had a moment revealed its charming outline against the lamp-lit interior, as she half

16

turned to close the door. Love has occasional metaphysical turns, and it was an odd feeling that came over him as he walked away, being nothing less than a rush of thankfulness and self-congratulation that he was not Madeline. For, if he had been she, he would have lost the ecstasy of loving her, of worshipping her. Ah, how much she lost, how much all those lose, who, fated to be the incarnations of beauty, goodness, and grace, are precluded from being their own worshippers! Well, it was a consolation that she didn't know it, that she actually thought that, with her little coquetries and exactions, she was enjoying the chief usufruct of her beauty. God make up to the haughty, wilful darling in some other way for missing the passing sweetness of the thrall she held her lovers in!

When Burr reached home, he found his sister Laura standing at the gate in a patch of moonlight.

"How pretty you look to-night!" he said, pinching her round cheek.

The young lady merely shrugged her shoulders, and replied dryly—

"So she let you go home with her."

"How do you know that?" he asked, laughing at her shrewd guess.

"Because you're so sweet, you goosey, of course."

But, in truth, any such mode of accounting for Henry's favourable comment on her appearance was quite unnecessary. Laura, with her petite, plump figure, sloe-black eyes, quick in moving, curly head, and dark, clear cheeks, carnation-tinted, would have been thought by many quite as charming a specimen of American girlhood as the stately pale brunette who swayed her brother's affections.

"Come for a walk, chicken! It is much too pretty a night to go indoors," he said.

"Yes, and furnish ears for Madeline's praises, with a few more reflected compliments for pay, perhaps," she replied, contemptuously. "Besides," she added, "I must go into the house and keep father company. I only came out to cool off after baking the cake. You'd better come in too. These moonlight nights always make him specially sad, you know."

The brother and sister had been left motherless not long before, and Laura, in trying to fill her mother's place in the household, so far as she might, was always looking out that her father should have as little opportunity as possible to brood alone over his companionless condition.

CHAPTER II

That same night toward morning Henry suddenly awoke from a sound sleep. Drowsiness, by some strange influence, had been completely banished from his eyes, and in its stead he became sensible of a profound depression of spirits. Physically, he was entirely comfortable, nor could he trace to any sensation from without either this sudden awakening or the mental condition in which he found himself. It was not that he thought of anything in particular that was gloomy or discouraging, but that all the ends and aims, not only of his own individual life, but of life in general, had assumed an aspect so empty, vain, and colourless, that he felt he would not rise from his bed for anything existence had to offer. He recalled his usual frame of mind, in which these things seemed attractive, with a dull wonderment that so baseless a delusion should be so strong and so general. He wondered if it were possible that it should ever again come over him.

The cold, grey light of earliest morning, that light which is rather the fading of night than the coming of day, filled the room with a faint hue, more cheerless than pitchiest darkness. A distant bell, with slow and heavy strokes, struck three. It was the dead point in the daily revolution of the earth's life, that point just before dawn, when men oftenest die; when surely, but for the force of momentum, the course of nature would stop, and at which doubtless it will one day pause eternally, when the clock is run down. The long-drawn reverberations of the bell, turning remoteness into music, full of the pathos of a sad and infinite patience, died away with an effect unspeakably dreary. His spirit, drawn forth after the vanishing vibrations, seemed to traverse waste spaces without beginning or ending, and aeons of monotonous duration. A sense of utter loneliness—loneliness inevitable, crushing, eternal, the loneliness of existence, encompassed by the infinite void of unconsciousness—enfolded him as a pall. Life lay like an incubus on his bosom. He shuddered at the thought that death might overlook him, and deny him its refuge. Even Madeline's face, as he conjured it up, seemed wan and pale, moving to unutterable pity, powerless to cheer, and all the illusions and passions of love were dim as ball-room candles in the grey light of dawn.

Gradually the moon passed, and he slept again.

As early as half-past eight the following forenoon, groups of men with very serious faces were to be seen standing at the corners of the streets, conversing in hushed tones, and women with awed voices were talking across the fences which divided adjoining yards. Even the children, as they went to school, forgot to play, and talked in whispers together, or lingered near the groups of men to catch a word or two of their conversation, or, maybe, walked silently along with a puzzled, solemn look upon their bright faces.

For a tragedy had occurred at dead of night which never had been paralleled in the history of the village. That morning the sun, as it peered through the closed shutters of an upper chamber, had relieved the darkness of a thing it had been afraid of. George Bayley sat there in a chair, his head sunk on his breast, a small, blue hole in his temple, whence a drop or two of blood had oozed, quite dead.

This, then, was what he meant when he said that he had made arrangements for leaving the village. The doctor thought that the fatal shot must have been fired about three o'clock that morning, and, when Henry heard this, he knew that it was the breath of the angel of death as he flew by that had chilled the genial current in his veins.

Bayley's family lived elsewhere, and his father, a stern, cold, haughty-looking man, was the only relative present at the funeral. When Mr. Lewis undertook to tell him, for his comfort, that there was reason to believe that George was out of his head when he took his life, Mr. Bayley interrupted him.

"Don't say that," he said. "He knew what he was doing. I should not wish any one to think otherwise. I am prouder of him than I had ever expected to be again."

A choir of girls with glistening eyes sang sweet, sad songs at the funeral, songs which, while they lasted, took away the ache of bereavement, like a cool sponge pressed upon a smarting spot. It seemed almost cruel that they must ever cease. And, after the funeral, the young men and girls who had known George, not feeling like returning that day to their ordinary thoughts and occupations, gathered at the house of one of them and passed the hours till dusk, talking tenderly of the departed, and recalling his generous traits and gracious ways.

The funeral had taken place on the day fixed for the picnic. The latter, in consideration of the saddened temper of the young people, was put off a fortnight.

CHAPTER III

About half-past eight on the morning of the day set for the postponed picnic, Henry knocked at Widow Brand's door. He had by no means forgotten Madeline's consent to allow him to carry her basket, although two weeks had intervened.

She came to the door herself. He had never seen her in anything that set off her dark eyes and olive complexion more richly than the simple picnic dress of white, trimmed with a little crimson braid about the neck and sleeves, which she wore to-day. It was gathered up at the bottom for wandering in the woods, just enough to show the little boots. She looked surprised at seeing him, and exclaimed—

"You haven't come to tell me that the picnic is put off again, or Laura's sick?"

"The picnic is all right, and Laura too. I've come to carry your basket for you."

"Why, you're really very kind," said she, as if she thought him slightly officious.

"Don't you remember you told me I might do so?" he said, getting a little red under her cool inspection.

"When did I?"

"Two weeks ago, that evening poor George spoke in meeting."

"Oh!" she answered, smiling, "so long ago as that? What a terrible memory you have! Come in just a moment, please; I'm nearly ready."

Whether she merely took his word for it, or whether she had remembered her promise perfectly well all the time, and only wanted to make him ask twice for the favour, lest he should feel too presumptuous, I don't pretend to know. Mrs. Brand set a chair for him with much cordiality. She was a gentle, mild-mannered little lady, such a contrast in style and character to Madeline that there was a certain amusing fitness in the latter's habit of calling her "My baby."

"You have a very pleasant day for your picnic, Mr. Burr," said she.

"Yes, we are very lucky," replied Henry, his eyes following Madeline's movements as she stood before the glass, putting on her hat, which had a red feather in it.

To have her thus add the last touches to her toilet in his presence was a suggestion of familiarity, of domesticity, that was very intoxicating to his imagination.

"Is your father well?" inquired Mrs. Brand, affably.

"Very well, thank you, very well indeed," he replied

"There; now I'm ready," said Madeline. "Here's the basket, Henry. Good-bye, mother."

They were a well-matched pair, the stalwart young man and the tall, graceful girl, and it is no wonder the girl's mother stood in the door looking after them with a thoughtful smile.

Hemlock Hollow was a glen between wooded bluffs, about a mile up the beautiful river on which Newville was situated, and boats had been collected at the rendezvous on the river-bank to convey the picnickers thither. On arriving, Madeline and Henry found all the party assembled and in capital spirits; There was still just enough shadow on their merriment to leave the disposition to laugh slightly in excess of its indulgence, than which no condition of mind more favourable to a good time can be imagined.

Laura was there, and to her Will Taylor had attached himself. He was a dapper little black-eyed fellow, a clerk in the dry-goods store, full of fun and good-nature, and a general favourite, but it was certainly rather absurd that Henry should be apprehensive of him as a rival. There also was Fanny Miller, who had the prettiest arm in Newville, a fact discovered once when she wore a Martha Washington toilet at a masquerade sociable, and since circulated from mouth to mouth among the young men. And there, too, was Emily Hunt, who had shocked the girls and thrown the youth into a pleasing panic by appearing at a young people's party the previous winter in low neck and short sleeves. It is to be remarked in extenuation that she had then but recently come from the city, and was not familiar with Newville etiquette. Nor must I forget to mention Ida Lewis, the minister's daughter, a little girl with poor complexion and beautiful brown eyes, who cherished a hopeless passion for Henry. Among the young men was Harry Tuttle, the clerk in the confectionery and fancy goods store, a young man whose father had once sent him for a term to a neighbouring seminary, as a result of which classical experience he still retained a certain jaunty student air verging on the rakish, that was admired by the girls and envied by the young men.

And there, above all, was Tom Longman. Tom was a big, hulking fellow, good-natured and simple-hearted in the extreme. He was the victim of an intense susceptibility to the girls' charms, joined with an intolerable shyness and self-consciousness when in their presence. From this consuming embarrassment he would seek relief by working like a horse whenever there was anything to do. With his hands

24

occupied he had an excuse for not talking to the girls or being addressed by them, and, thus shielded from the, direct rays of their society, basked with inexpressible emotions in the general atmosphere of sweetness and light which they diffused. He liked picnics because there was much work to do, and never attended indoor parties because there was none. This inordinate taste for industry in connection with social enjoyment on Tom's part was strongly encouraged by the other young men, and they were the ones who always stipulated that he should be of the party when there was likely to be any call for rowing, taking care of horses, carrying of loads, putting out of croquet sets, or other manual exertion. He was generally an odd one in such companies. It would be no kindness to provide him a partner, and, besides, everybody made so many jokes about him that none of the girls quite cared to have their names coupled with his, although they all had a compassionate liking for him.

On the present occasion this poor slave of the petticoat had been at work preparing the boats all the morning.

"Why, how nicely you have arranged everything!" said Madeline kindly, as she stood on the sand waiting for Henry to bring up a boat.

"What?" replied Tom, laughing in a flustered way.

He always laughed just so and said "what?" when any of the girls spoke to him, being too much confused by the fact of being addressed to catch what was said the first time.

"It's very good of you to arrange the boats for us, Madeline repeated.

"Oh, 'tain't anything, 'tain't anything at all," he blurted out, with a very red face.

"You are going up in our boat, ain't you, Longman?" said Harry Tuttle.

"No, Tom, you're going with us," cried another young man.

"He's going with us, like a sensible fellow," said Will Taylor, who, with Laura Burr, was sitting on the forward thwart of the boat, into the stern of which Henry was now assisting Madeline.

"Tom, these lazy young men are just wanting you to do their rowing for them," said she. "Get into our boat, and I'll make Henry row you."

"What do you say to that, Henry?" said Tom, snickering.

"It isn't for me to say anything after Madeline has spoken," replied the young man.

"She has him in good subjection," remarked Ida Lewis, not over-sweetly.

"All right, I'll come in your boat, Miss Brand, if you'll take care of me," said Tom, with a sudden spasm of boldness, followed by violent blushes at the thought that perhaps be had said something too free. The boat was pushed off. Nobody took the oars.

"I thought you were going to row?" said Madeline, turning to Henry, who sat beside her in the stern.

"Certainly," said he, making as if he would rise. "Tom, you just sit here while I row."

"Oh no, I'd just as lief row," said Tom, seizing the oars with feverish haste.

"So would I, Tom; I want a little exercise," urged Henry with a hypocritical grin, as he stood up in an attitude of readiness.

"Oh, I like to row. 'I'd a great deal rather. Honestly," asseverated Tom, as he made the water foam with the violence of his strokes, compelling Henry to resume his seat to preserve his equilibrium.

"It's perfectly plain that you don't want to sit by me, Tom. That hurts my feelings," said Madeline, pretending to pout.

"Oh no, it isn't that," protested Tom. "Only I'd rather row; that is, I mean, you know, it's such fun rowing."

"Very well, then," said Madeline, "I sha'n't help you any more; and here they all are tying their boats on to ours."

Sure enough, one of the other boats had fastened its chain to the stern of theirs, and the others had fastened to that; their oarsmen were lying off and Tom was propelling the entire flotilla.

"Oh, I can row 'em all just as easy's not," gasped the devoted youth, the perspiration rolling down his forehead.

But this was a little too bad, and Henry soon cast off the other boats, in spite of the protests of their occupants, who regarded Tom's brawn and muscle as the common stock of the entire party, which no one boat had a right to appropriate.

On reaching Hemlock Hollow, Madeline asked the poor young man for his hat, and returned it to him adorned with evergreens, which nearly distracted him with bashfulness and delight, and drove him to seek a safety-valve for his excitement in superhuman activity all the rest of the morning, arranging croquet sets, hanging swings, breaking ice, squeezing lemons, and fetching water.

"Oh, how thirsty I am!" sighed Madeline, throwing down her croquet mallet.

"The ice-water is not yet ready, but I know a spring a little way off where the water is cold as ice," said Henry.

"Show it to me this instant," she cried, and they walked off together, followed by Ida Lewis's unhappy eyes.

The distance to the spring was not great, but the way was rough, and once or twice he had to help her over fallen trees and steep banks. Once she slipped a little, and for, a single supreme moment he held her whole weight in his arms. Before, they had been talking and laughing gaily, but that made a sudden silence. He dared not look at her for some moments, and when he did there was a slight flush tingeing her usually colourless cheek.

His pulses were already bounding wildly, and, at this betrayal that she had shared his consciousness at that moment, his agitation was tenfold increased. It was the first time she had ever shown a sign of confusion in his presence. The sensation

27

of mastery, of power over her, which it gave, was so utterly new that it put a sort of madness in his blood. Without a word they came to the spring and pretended to drink. As she turned to go back, he lightly caught her fingers in a detaining clasp, and said, in a voice rendered harsh by suppressed emotion—

"Don't be in such a hurry. Where will you find a cooler spot?"

"Oh, it's cool enough anywhere! Let's go back," she replied, starting to return as she spoke. She saw his excitement, and, being herself a little confused, had no idea of allowing a scene to be precipitated just then. She flitted on before with so light a foot that he did not overtake her until she came to a bank too steep for her to surmount without aid. He sprang up and extended her his hand. Assuming an expression as if she were unconscious who was helping her, she took it, and he drew her up to his side. Then with a sudden, audacious impulse, half hoping she would not be angry, half reckless if she were, he clasped her closely in his arms, and kissed her lips. She gasped, and freed herself.

"How dared you do such a thing to me?" she cried.

The big fellow stood before her, sheepish, dogged, contrite, desperate, all in one.

"I couldn't help it," he blurted out. The plea was somehow absurdly simple, and yet rather unanswerable. Angry as she was, she really couldn't think of anything to say, except—

"You'd better help it," with which rather ineffective rebuke she turned away and walked toward the picnic ground. Henry followed in a demoralized frame. His mind was in a ferment. He could not realize what had happened. He could scarcely believe that he had actually done it. He could not conceive how he had dared it. And now what penalty would she inflict? What if she should not forgive him? His soul was dissolved in fears. But, sooth to say, the young lady's actual state of mind was by no means so implacable as he apprehended. She had been ready to be very angry, but the suddenness and depth of his contrition had disarmed her. It took all the force out of her indignation to see that he actually seemed to have a deeper sense of the enormity of his act than she herself had. And when, after they had rejoined the party, she saw that, instead of taking part in the sports, he kept aloof, wandering aimless and disconsolate by himself among the pines, she took compassion on him and sent some one to tell him she wanted him to come and push her in the swing. People had kissed her before. She was not going to leave the first person who had seemed to fully realize the importance of the proceeding to suffer unduly from a susceptibility which did him so much credit. As for Henry, he hardly believed his ears when he heard the summons to attend her. At that the kiss which her rebuke had turned cold on his lips began to glow afresh, and for the first time he tasted its exceeding sweetness; for her calling to him seemed to ratify and consent to it. There were others standing about as he came up to where Madeline sat in the swing, and he was silent, for he could not talk of indifferent things.

With what a fresh charm, with what new sweet suggestions of complaisance that kiss had invested every line and curve of her, from hat-plume to boot-tip! A delicious tremulous sense of proprietorship tinged his every thought of her. He touched the swing-rope as fondly as if it were an electric chain that could communicate the caress to her. Tom Longman, having done all the work that offered itself, had been wandering about in a state of acute embarrassment, not daring to join himself to any of the groups, much less accost a young lady who might be alone. As he drifted near the swing, Madeline said to Henry—

"You may stop swinging me now. I think I'd like to go out rowing." The young man's cup seemed running over. He could scarcely command his voice for delight as he said—

"It will be jolly rowing just now. I'm sure we can get some pond-lilies."

29

"Really," she replied, airily, "you take too much for granted. I was going to ask Tom Longman to take me out."

She called to Tom, and as he came up, grinning and shambling, she indicated to him her pleasure that he should row her upon the river. The idea of being alone in a small boat for perhaps fifteen minutes with the belle of Newville, and the object of his own secret and distant adoration, paralysed Tom's faculties with an agony of embarrassment. He grew very red, and there was such a buzzing in his ears that he could not feel sure he heard aright, and Madeline had to repeat herself several times before he seemed to fully realize the appalling nature of the proposition. As they walked down to the shore she chatted with him, but he only responded with a profusion of vacant laughs. When he had pulled out on the river, his rowing, from his desire to make an excuse for not talking, was so tremendous that they cheered him from the shore, at the same time shouting—

"Keep her straight! You're going into the bank!"

The truth was, that Tom could not guide the boat because he did not dare to look astern for fear of meeting Madeline's eyes, which, to judge from the space his eyes left around her, he must have supposed to fill at least a quarter of the horizon, like an aurora, in fact. But, all the same, he was having an awfully good time, although perhaps it would be more proper to say he would have a good time when he came to think it over afterward. It was an experience which would prove a mine of gold in his memory, rich enough to furnish for years the gilding to his modest day-dreams. Beauty, like wealth, should make its owners generous. It is a gracious thing in fair women at times to make largesse of their beauty, bestowing its light more freely on tongue-tied, timid adorers than on their bolder suitors, giving to them who dare not ask. Their beauty never can seem more precious to women than when for charity's sake they brighten with its lustre the eyes of shy and retiring admirers.

As Henry was ruefully meditating upon the uncertainty of the sex, and debating the probability that Madeline had called him to swing her for the express purpose of getting a chance to snub him, Ida Lewis came to him, and said—

"Mr. Burr, we're getting up a game of croquet. Won't you play?"

"If I can be on your side," he answered, civilly.

He knew the girl's liking for him, and was always kind to her. At his answer her face flushed with pleasure, and she replied shyly—

"If you'd like to, you may."

Henry was not in the least a conceited fellow, but it was impossible that he should not understand the reason why Ida, who all the morning had looked forlorn enough, was now the life of the croquet-ground, and full of smiles and flushes. She was a good player, and had a corresponding interest in beating, but her equanimity on the present occasion was not in the least disturbed by the disgraceful defeat which Henry's awkwardness and absence of mind entailed on their aide.

But her portion of sunshine for that day was brief enough, for Madeline soon returned from her boat-ride, and Henry found an excuse for leaving the game and joining her where she sat on the ground between the knees of a gigantic oak sorting pond-lilies, which the girls were admiring. As he came up, she did not appear to notice him. As soon as he had a chance to speak without being overheard, he said, soberly—

"Tom ought to thank me for that boat-ride, I suppose."

"I don't know what you mean," she answered, with assumed carelessness.

"I mean that you went to punish me."

"You're sufficiently conceited," she replied. "Laura, come here; your brother is teasing me."

"And do you think I want to be teased to?" replied that young lady, pertly, as she walked off.

Madeline would have risen and left Henry, but she was too proud to let him think that she was afraid of him.. Neither was she afraid, but she was confused, and momentarily without her usual self-confidence. One reason for her running off with Tom had been to get a chance to think. No girl, however coolly her blood may flow, can be pressed to a man's breast, wildly throbbing with love for her, and not experience some agitation in consequence. Whatever may be the state of her sentiments, there is a magnetism in such a contact which she cannot at once throw off. That kiss had brought her relations with Henry to a crisis. It had precipitated the necessity of some decision. She could no longer hold him off, and play with him. By that bold dash he had gained a vantage-ground, a certain masterful attitude which he had never held before. Yet, after all, I am not sure that she was not just a little afraid of him, and, moreover, that she did not like him all the better for it. It was such a novel feeling that it began to make some things, thought of in connection with him, seem more possible to her mind than they had ever seemed before. As she peeped furtively at this young man, so suddenly grown formidable, as he reclined carelessly on the ground at her feet, she admitted to herself that there was something very manly in the sturdy figure and square forehead, with the curly black locks hanging over it. She looked at him with a new interest, half shrinking, half attracted, as one who might come into a very close relation with herself. She scarcely knew whether the thought was agreeable or not.

"Give me your hat," she said, "and I'll put some lilies in it."

"You are very good," said he, handing it to her.

"Does it strike you so?" she replied, hesitatingly. "Then I won't do it. I don't want to appear particularly good to you. I didn't know just how it would seem."

"Oh, it won't seem very good; only about middling," he urged, upon which representation she took the hat.

He watched her admiringly as she deftly wreathed the lilies around it, holding it up, now this way and now that, while she critically inspected the effect.

Then her caprice changed. "I've half a mind to drop it into the river. Would you jump after it?" she said, twirling it by the brim, and looking over the steep bank, near which she sat, into the deep, dark water almost perpendicularly below.

"If it were anything of yours instead of mine, I would jump quickly enough," he replied.

She looked at him with a reckless gleam in her eyes.

"You mustn't talk chaff to me, sir; we'll see," and, snatching a glove from her pocket, she held it out over the water. They were both of them in that state of suppressed excitement which made such an experiment on each other's nerve dangerous. Their eyes met, and neither flinched. If she had dropped it, he would have gone after it.

"After all," she said, suddenly, "that would be taking a good deal of trouble to get a mitten. If you are so anxious for it, I will give it to you now;" and she held out the glove to him with an inscrutable face.

He sprang up from the ground. "Madeline, do you mean it?" he asked, scarcely audibly, his face grown white and pinched. She crumpled the obnoxious glove into her pocket.

"Why, you poor fellow!" she exclaimed, the wildfire in her eyes quenched in a moment with the dew of pity. "Do you care so much?"

"I care everything," he said, huskily.

But, as luck would have it, just at that instant Will Taylor came running up, pursued by Laura, and threw himself upon Madeline's protection. It appeared that he had confessed to the possession of a secret, and on being requested by Laura to impart it had flatly refused to do so.

"I can't really interfere to protect any young man who refuses to tell a secret to a young lady," said Madeline, gravely. "Neglect to tell her the secret, without being particularly asked to do so, would be bad enough, but to refuse after being requested is an offence which calls for the sharpest correction."

"And that isn't all, either," said Laura, vindictively flirting the switch with which she had pursued him. "He used offensive language."

"What did he say?" demanded Madeline, judicially.

"I asked him if he was sure it was a secret that I didn't know already, and he said he was; and I asked him what made him sure, and he said because if I knew it everybody else would. As much as to say I couldn't keep a secret."

"This looks worse and worse, young man," said the judge, severely. "The only course left for you is to make a clean breast of the affair, and throw yourself on the mercy of the court. If the secret turns out to be a good one, I'll let you off as easily as I can."

"It's about the new drug-clerk, the one who is going to take George Bayley's place," said Will, laughing.

"Oh, do tell, quick!" exclaimed Laura.

"I don't care who it is. I sha'n't like him," said Madeline. "Poor George! and here we are forgetting all about him this beautiful day!"

"What's the new clerk's name?" said Laura, impatiently.

"Harrison Cordis."

"What?"

"Harrison Cordis."

"Rather an odd name," said Laura. "I never heard it."

"No," said Will; "he comes all the way from Boston."

"Is he handsome?" inquired Laura.

"I really don't know," replied Will. "I presume Parker failed to make that a condition, although really he ought to, for the looks of the clerk is the principal element in the sale of soda-water, seeing girls are the only ones who drink it."

"Of course it is," said Laura, frankly. "I didn't drink any all last summer, because poor George's sad face took away my disposition. Never mind," she added, "we shall all have a chance to see how he looks at church to-morrow;" and with that the two girls went off together to help set the table for lunch.

The picnickers did not row home till sunset, but Henry found no opportunity to resume the conversation with Madeline which had been broken off at such an interesting point.

CHAPTER IV

The advent of a stranger was an event of importance in the small social world of Newville. Mr. Harrison Cordis, the new clerk in the drug-store, might well have been flattered by the attention which he excited at church the next day, especially from the fairer half of the congregation. Far, however, from appearing discomposed thereby, he returned it with such interest that at least half the girls thought they had captivated him by the end of the morning service. They all agreed that he was awfully handsome, though Laura maintained that he was rather too pretty for a man. He was certainly very pretty. His figure was tall, slight, and elegant. He had delicate hands and feet, a white forehead, deep blue, smiling eyes, short, curly, yellow, hair, and a small moustache, drooping over lips as enticing as a girl's. But the ladies voted his manners yet more pleasing than his appearance. They were charmed by his easy self-possession, and constant alertness as to details of courtesy. The village beaus scornfully called him "cityfied," and secretly longed to be like him. A shrewder criticism than that to which he was exposed would, however, have found the fault with Cordis's manners that, under a show of superior ease and affability, he was disposed to take liberties with his new acquaintances, and exploit their simplicity for his own entertainment. Evidently he felt that he was in the country.

That very first Sunday, after evening meeting, he induced Fanny Miller, at whose father's house he boarded, to introduce him to Madeline, and afterward walked home with her, making himself very agreeable, and crowning his audacity by asking permission to call. Fanny, who went along with them, tattled of this, and it produced a considerable sensation among the girls, for it was the wont of Newville wooers to make very gradual approaches. Laura warmly expressed to Madeline her indignation at the impudence of the proceeding, but that young lady was sure she did not see any harm in it; whereupon Laura lost her temper a little, and hinted that it might be more to her credit if she did. Madeline replied pointedly, and the result was a little spat, from which Laura issued second best, as people generally did who provoked a verbal strife with Madeline. Meanwhile it was rumoured that Cordis had availed himself of the permission that he had asked, and that he had, moreover, been seen talking with her in the post-office several times.

The drug-store being next door to the post-office, it was easy for him, under pretence of calling for the mail, to waylay there any one he might wish to meet. The last of the week Fanny Miller gave a little tea-party, to make Cordis more generally acquainted. On that occasion he singled out Madeline with his attentions in such a pronounced manner that the other girls were somewhat piqued. Laura, having her brother's interest at heart, had much more serious reasons for being uneasy at the look of things. They all remarked how queerly Madeline acted that evening. She was so subdued and quiet, not a bit like herself. When the party broke up, Cordis walked home with Madeline and Laura, whose paths lay together.

37

"I'm extremely fortunate," said he, as he was walking on with Laura, after leaving Madeline at her house, "to have a chance to escort the two belles of Newville at once."

"I'm not so foolish as I look, Mr. Cordis," said she, rather sharply. She was not going to let him think he could turn the head of every Newville girl as he had Madeline's with his city airs and compliments.

"You might be, and not mind owning it," he replied, making an excuse of her words to scrutinise her face with a frank admiration that sent the colour to her cheeks, though she was more vexed than pleased.

"I mean that I don't like flattery."

"Are you sure?" he asked, with apparent surprise.

"Of course I am. What a question!"

"Excuse me; I only asked because I never met any one before who didn't."

"Never met anybody who didn't like to be told things about themselves which they knew weren't true, and were just said because somebody thought they were foolish enough to believe 'em?"

"I don't expect you to believe 'em yourself," he replied; "only vain people believe the good things people say about them; but I wouldn't give a cent for friends who didn't think better of me than I think of myself, and tell me so occasionally, too."

They stood a moment at Laura's gate, and just then Henry, coming home from the gun-shop of which he was foreman, passed them, and entered the house. "Is that your brother?" asked Cordis.

"Yes."

"It does one's eyes good to see such a powerful looking young man. Is your brother married, may I ask?"

"He is not."

"In coming into a new circle as I have done, you understand, Miss Burr, I often feel a certain awkwardness on account of

38

not knowing the relations between the persons I meet," he said, apologizing for his questions.

Laura saw her opportunity, and promptly improved it.

"My brother has been attentive to Miss Brand for a long time. They are about as good as engaged. Good-evening, Mr. Cordis."

It so happened that several days after this conversation, as Madeline was walking home one afternoon, she glanced back at a crossing of the street, and saw Harrison Cordis coming behind her on his way to tea. At the rate she was walking she would reach home before he overtook her, but, if she walked a very little slower, he would overtake her. Her pace slackened. She blushed at her conduct, but she did not hurry.

The most dangerous lovers women have are men of Cordis's feminine temperament. Such men, by the delicacy and sensitiveness of their own organizations, read women as easily and accurately as women read each other. They are alert to detect and interpret those smallest trifles in tone, expression, and bearing, which betray the real mood far more unmistakably than more obvious signs. Cordis had seen her backward glance, and noted her steps grow slower with a complacent smile. It was this which emboldened him, in spite of the short acquaintance, to venture on the line he did.

"Good-evening, Miss Brand," he said, as he over took her. "I don't really think it's fair to begin to hurry when you hear somebody trying to overtake you.

"I'm sure I didn't mean to," she replied, glad to have a chance to tell the truth, without suspecting, poor girl, that he knew very well she was telling it.

"It isn't safe to," he said, laughing. "You can't tell who it may be. Now, it might have been Mr. Burr, instead of only me."

She understood instantly. Somebody had been telling him about Henry's attentions to her. A bitter anger, a feeling of which a moment before she would have deemed herself utterly incapable, surged up in her heart against the person, whoever it was, who had told him this. For several seconds she could not control herself to speak. Finally, she said—

"I don't understand you. Why do you speak of Mr. Burr to me?"

"I beg pardon. I should not have done so."

"Please explain what you mean.

"You'll excuse me, I hope," he said, as if quite distressed to have displeased her. "It was an unpardonable indiscretion on my part, but somebody told me, or at least I understood, that you were engaged to him."

"Somebody has told you a falsehood, then," she replied, and, with a bow of rather strained dignity turned in at the gate of a house where a moment before she had not had the remotest intention of stopping. If she had been in a boat with him, she would have jumped into the water sooner than protract the inter-view a moment after she had said that. Mechanically she walked up the path and knocked at the door. Until the lady of the house opened it, she did not notice where she had stopped.

Good-afternoon, Madeline. I'm glad to see you. You haven't made me a call this ever so long."

"I'm sorry, Mrs. Tuttle, but I haven't time to stop to-day. Ha—have you got a—a pattern of a working apron? I'd like to borrow it."

CHAPTER V

Now, Henry had not chanced to be at church that first Sunday evening when Cordis obtained an introduction to Madeline, nor was he at Fanny Miller's teaparty. Of the rapidly progressing flirtation between his sweetheart and the handsome drug-clerk he had all this time no suspicion whatever. Spending his days from dawn to sunset in the shop among men, he was not in the way of hearing gossip on that sort of subject; and Laura, who ordinarily kept him posted on village news, had, deemed it best to tell him as yet nothing of her apprehensions. She was aware that the affection between her brother and Madeline was chiefly on his side, and knew enough of her wilfulness to be sure that any attempted interference by him would only make matters worse. Moreover, now that she had warned Cordis that Madeline was pre-empted property, she hoped he would turn his attention elsewhere.

And so, while half the village was agog over the flirtation of the new drug-clerk with Madeline Brand, and Laura was lying awake nights fretting about it, Henry went gaily to and from his work in a state of blissful ignorance. And it was very blissful. He was exultant over the progress he had made in his courtship at the picnic. He had told his love—he had kissed her. If he had not been accepted, he had, at least, not been rejected, and that was a measure of success quite enough to intoxicate so ardent and humble a lover as he. And, indeed, what lover might not have taken courage at remembering the sweet pity that shone in her eyes at the revelation of his love-lorn state? The fruition of his hopes, to which he had only dared look forward as possibly awaiting him somewhere in the dim future, was, maybe, almost at hand. Circumstances combined to prolong these rose-tinted dreams. A sudden press of orders made it necessary to run the shop till late nights. He contrived with difficulty to get out early one evening so as to call on Madeline; but she had gone out, and he failed to see her. It was some ten days after the picnic that, on calling a second time, he found her at home. It chanced to be the very evening of the day on which the conversation between Madeline and Cordis, narrated in the last chapter, had taken place.

She did not come in till Henry had waited some time in the parlour, and then gave him her hand in a very lifeless way. She said she had a bad head-ache, and seemed disposed to leave the talking to him. He spoke of the picnic, but she rather sharply remarked that it was so long ago that she had forgotten all about it. It did seem very long ago to her, but to him it was very fresh. This cool ignoring of all that had happened that day in modifying their relations at one blow knocked the bottom out of all his thinking for the past week, and left him, as it were, all in the air. While he felt that the moment was not propitious for pursuing that topic, he could not for the moment turn his mind to anything else, and, as for Madeline, it appeared to be a matter of entire indifference to her whether anything further was said on any subject. Finally, he remarked, with an effort to which the result may appear disproportionate—

"Mr. Taylor has been making quite extensive alterations on his house, hasn't he?"

"I should think you ought to know, if any one. You pass his house every day," was her response.

"Why, of course I know," he said, staring at her.

"So I thought, but you said 'hasn't he?' And naturally I presumed that you were not quite certain."

She was evidently quizzing him, but her face was inscrutable. She looked only as if patiently and rather wearily explaining a misunderstanding. As she played with her fan, she had an unmistakable expression of being slightly bored.

"Madeline, do you know what I should say was the matter with you if you' were a man?" he said, desperately, yet trying to laugh.

"Well, really"—and her eyes had a rather hard expression—"if you prefer gentlemen's society, you'd better seek it, instead of trying to get along by supposing me to be a gentleman."

"It seems as if I couldn't say anything right," said Henry.

"I think you do talk a little strangely," she admitted, with a faint smile. Her look was quite like that of an uncomplaining martyr.

"What's the matter with you to-night, Madeline? Tell me, for God's sake!" he cried, overcome with sudden grief and alarm.

"I thought I told you I had a headache, and I really wish you wouldn't use profane language," she replied, regarding him with lack-lustre eyes.

"And that's all? It's only a headache?"

"That's quite enough, I'm sure. Would you like me to have toothache besides?"

"You know I didn't mean that."

"Well, earache, then?" she said, wearily, allowing her head to rest back on the top of her chair, as if it were too much of an effort to hold it up, and half shutting her eyes.

"Excuse me, I ought not to have kept you. I'll go now.'

"Don't hurry," she observed, languidly.

"I hope you'll feel better in the morning."

He offered her his hand, and she put hers in his for an instant, but withdrew it without returning his pressure, and he went away, sorely perplexed and bitterly disappointed.

He would have been still more puzzled if he had been told that not only had Madeline not forgotten about what had happened at the picnic, but had, in fact, thought of scarcely anything else during his call. It was that which made her so hard with him, that lent such acid to her tone and such cold aversion to her whole manner. As he went from the house, she stood looking after him through the parlour window, murmuring to herself—.

"Thank Heaven, I'm not engaged to him. How could I think I would ever marry him? Oh, if a girl only knew!"

Henry could not rest until he had seen her again, and found out whether her coldness was a mere freak of coquetry, or something more. One evening when, thanks to the long twilight, it was not yet dark, he called again. She came to the door with hat and gloves on. Was she going out? he asked. She admitted that she had been on the point of going across the street to make a call which had been too long delayed, but wouldn't he come in. No, he would not detain her; he would call again. But he lingered a moment on the steps while, standing on the threshold, she played with a button of a glove. Suddenly he raised his eyes and regarded her in a quite particular manner. She was suddenly absorbed with her glove, but he fancied that her cheek slightly flushed. Just at the moment when he was calculating that she could no longer well avoid looking up, she exclaimed—

"Dear me, how vexatious! there goes another of those buttons. I shall have to sew it on again before I go," and she looked at him with a charmingly frank air of asking for sympathy, at the same time that it conveyed the obvious idea that she ought to lose no time in making the necessary repairs.

"I will not keep you, then," he said, somewhat sadly, and turned away.

Was the accident intentional? Did she want to avoid him? he could not help the thought, and yet what could be more frank and sunshiny than the smile with which she responded to his parting salutation?

The next Sunday Laura and he were at church in the evening.

"I wonder why Madeline was not out. Do you know?" he said as they were walking home.

"No."

"You're not nearly so friendly with her as you used to be. What's the matter?"

She did not reply, for just then at a turning of the street, they met the young lady of whom they were speaking. She looked smiling and happy, and very handsome, with a flush in either cheek, and walking with her was the new drug-clerk. She seemed a little confused at meeting Henry, and for a moment appeared to avoid his glance. Then, with a certain bravado, oddly mingled with a deprecating air, she raised her eyes to his and bowed.

It was the first intimation he had had of the true reason of her alienation. Mechanically he walked on and on, too stunned to think as yet, feeling only that there was a terrible time of thinking ahead.

"Hadn't we better turn back, hear?" said Laura, very gently.

He looked up. They were a mile or two out of the village on a lonely country road. They turned, and she said, softly, in the tone like the touch of tender fingers on an aching spot—

"I knew it long ago, but I hadn't the heart to tell you. She set her cap at him from the first. Don't take it too much to heart. She is not good enough for you."

45

Sweet compassion! Idle words! Is there any such sense of ownership, reaching even to the feeling of identity, as that which the lover has in the one he loves? His thoughts and affections, however short the time, had so grown about her and encased her, as the hardened clay imbeds the fossil flower buried ages ago. It rather seems as if he had found her by quarrying in the depths of his own heart than as if he had picked her from the outside world, from among foreign things. She was never foreign, else he could not have had that intuitive sense of intimateness with her which makes each new trait which she reveals, while a sweet surprise, yet seem in a deeper sense familiar, as if answering to some pre-existing ideal pattern in his own heart, as if it were something that could not have been different. In after years he may grow rich in land and gold, but he never again will have such sense of absolute right and eternally foreordained ownership in any thing as he had long years ago in that sweet girl whom some other fellow married. For, alas! this seemingly inviolable divine title is really no security at all. Love is liable to ten million suits for breach of warranty. The title-deeds he gives to lovers, taking for price their hearts' first-fruits, turn out no titles at all. Half the time, title to the same property is given to several claimants, and the one to finally take possession is often enough one who has no title from love at all.

Henry had been hit hard, but there was a dogged persistence in his disposition that would not allow him to give up till he had tested his fortune to the uttermost. His love was quite unmixed with vanity, for Madeline had never given him any real reason to think that she loved him, and, therefore, the risk of an additional snub or two counted for nothing to deter him. The very next day he left the shop in the afternoon and called on her. Her rather constrained and guarded manner was as if she thought he had come to call her to account, and was prepared for him. He, on the contrary, tried to look as affable and well satisfied as if he were the most prosperous of lovers. When he asked her if she would go out driving with him that afternoon, she was evidently taken quite off her guard. For recrimination she was prepared, but not for this smiling proposal. But she recovered herself in an instant, and said—

"I'm really very much obliged. It is very considerate of you, but my mother is not very well this afternoon, and I feel that I ought not to leave her." Smothering a sick feeling of discouragement, he said, as cheerfully as possible—

"I'm very sorry indeed. Is your mother seriously sick?"

"Oh no, thank you. I presume she will be quite well by morning."

"Won't you, perhaps, go to-morrow afternoon, if she is better? The river road which you admire so much is in all its midsummer glory."

"Thank you. Really; you are quite too good, but I think riding is rather likely to give me the headache lately."

The way she answered him, without being in the least uncivil, left the impression on his mind that he had been duly persistent. There was an awkward silence of a few moments, and he was just about to burst forth with he knew not what exclamations and entreaties, when Madeline rose, saying—

"Excuse me a moment; I think I hear my mother calling," and left the room.

She was gone some time, and returned and sat down with an absent and preoccupied expression of face, and he did not linger.

The next Thursday evening he was at conference meeting, intending to walk home with Madeline if she would let him; to ask her, at least. She was there, as usual, and sat at the melodeon. A few minutes before nine Cordis came in, evidently for the mere purpose of escorting her home. Henry doggedly resolved that she should choose between them then and there, before all the people. The closing hymn was sung, and the buzz of the departing congregation sounded in his ears as if it were far away. He rose and took his place near the door, his face pale, his lips set, regardless of all observers. Cordis, with whom he was unacquainted save by sight, stood near by, good-humouredly smiling, and greeting the people as they passed out.

In general, Madeline liked well enough the excitement of electing between rival suitors, but she would rather, far rather, have avoided this public choice tonight. She had begun to be sorry for Henry. She was as long as possible about closing the melodeon. She opened and closed it again. At length, finding no further excuse for delaying, she came slowly down the aisle, looking a little pale herself. Several of the village young folks who understood the situation lingered, smiling at one other, to see the fun out, and Cordis himself recognized his rival's tragical look with an amused expression, at the same time that he seemed entirely disposed to cross lances with him.

As Madeline approached the door, Henry stepped forward and huskily asked if he might take her home. Bowing to him with a gracious smile of declination, she said, "Thanks," and, taking Cordis's arm, passed out with him.

As they came forth into the shadow of the night, beyond the illumination of the porch lamps of the church, Cordis observed—

"Really, that was quite tragical. I half expected he would pull out a revolver and shoot us both. Poor fellow, I'm sorry for him."

"He was sorrier than you are glad, I dare say, said Madeline.

"Well, I don't know about that," he replied; "I'm as glad as I can be, and I suppose he's as sorry as he can be. I can't imagine any man in love with such a girl as you not being one or the other all the while."

But the tone was a little, a very little, colder than the words, and her quick ear caught the difference.

"What's the matter? Are you vexed about anything? What have I done?" she asked, in a tone of anxious deprecation

48

which no other person but Harrison Cordis had ever heard from her lips.

"You have done nothing," he answered, passing his arm round her waist in a momentary embrace of reassurance. "It is I that am ill-tempered. I couldn't help thinking from the way this Burr pursues you that there must have been something in the story about your having been engaged, after all."

"It is not true. I never was engaged. I couldn't bear him. I don't like him. Only he—he—"

"I don't want to pry into your secrets. Don't make any confessions to me. I have no right to call you to account," he interrupted her, rather stiffly.

"Please don't say that. Oh, please don't talk that way!" she cried out, as if the words had hurt her like a knife. "He liked me, but I didn't like him. I truly didn't. Don't you believe me? What shall I do if you don't?"

It must not be supposed that Cordis had inspired so sudden and strong a passion in Madeline without a reciprocal sentiment. He had been infatuated from the first with the brilliant, beautiful girl, and his jealousy was at least half real. Her piteous distress at his slight show of coldness melted him to tenderness. There was an impassioned reconciliation, to which poor Henry was the sacrifice. Now that he threatened to cost her the smiles of the man she loved, her pity for him was changed into resentment. She said to herself that it was mean and cruel in him to keep pursuing her. It never occurred to her to find Cordis's conduct unfair in reproaching her for not having lived solely for him, before she knew even of his existence. She was rather inclined to side with him, and blame herself for having lacked an intuitive prescience of his coming, which should have kept her a nun in heart and soul.

The next evening, about dusk, Henry was wandering sadly and aimlessly about the streets when he met Madeline face to face. At first she seemed rather unpleasantly startled, and made as if she would pass him without giving him an opportunity to speak to her. Then she appeared to change

49

her mind, and, stopping directly before him, said, in a low voice—

"Won't you please leave me alone, after this? Your attentions are not welcome."

Without giving him a chance to reply, she passed on and walked swiftly up the street. He leaned against the fence, and stood motionless for a long time. That was all that was wanting to make his loss complete—an angry word from her. At last his lips moved a little, and slowly formed these words in a husky, very pitiful whisper—

"That's the end,"

CHAPTER VI

There was one person, at least, in the village who had viewed the success of the new drug-clerk in carrying off the belle of Newville with entire complacency, and that was Ida Lewis, the girl with a poor complexion and beautiful brown eyes, who had cherished a rather hopeless inclination for Henry; now that he had lost that bold girl, she tremulously assured herself, perhaps it was not quite so hopeless. Laura, too, had an idea that such might possibly be the case, and hoping at least to distract her brother, about whom she was becoming quite anxious, she had Ida over to tea once or twice, and, by various other devices which with a clever woman are matters of course, managed to throw her in his way.

He was too much absorbed to take any notice of this at first, but, one evening when Ida was at tea with them, it suddenly flashed upon him, and his face reddened with annoyed embarrassment. He had never felt such a cold anger at Laura as at that moment. He had it in his heart to say something very bitter to her. Would she not at least respect his grief?

51

He had ado to control the impulse that prompted him to rise and leave the table. And then, with that suddenness characteristic of highly wrought moods, his feelings changed, and he discovered how soft-hearted his own sorrow had made him toward all who suffered in the same way. His eyes smarted with pitifulness as he noted the pains with which the little girl opposite him had tried to make the most of her humble charms in the hope of catching his eye. And the very poverty of those charms made her efforts the more pathetic. He blamed his eyes for the hard clearness with which they noted the shortcomings of the small, unformed features, the freckled skin, the insignificant and niggardly contour, and for the cruelty of the comparison they suggested between all this and Madeline's rich beauty. A boundless pity poured out of his heart to cover and transfigure these defects, and he had an impulse to make up to her for them, if he could, by sacrificing himself to her, if she desired. If she felt toward him as he toward Madeline, it were worth his life to save the pity of another such heart-breaking. So should he atone, perhaps, for the suffering Madeline had given him.

After tea he went by himself to nurse these wretched thoughts, and although the sight of Ida had suggested them, he went on to think of himself, and soon became so absorbed in his own misery that he quite forgot about her, and, failing to rejoin the girls that evening, Ida had to go home alone, which was a great disappointment to her. But it was, perhaps, quite as well, on the whole, for both of them that he was not thrown with her again that evening.

It is never fair to take for granted that the greatness of a sorrow or a loss is a just measure of the fault of the one who causes it. Madeline was not willingly cruel. She felt sorry in a way for Henry whenever his set lips and haggard face came under her view, but sorry in a dim and distant way, as one going on a far and joyous journey is sorry for the former associates he leaves behind, associates whose faces already, ere he goes, begin to grow faded and indistinct. At the wooing of Cordis her heart had awaked, and in the high, new joy of loving, she scorned the tame delight of being loved, which, until then, had been her only idea of the passion.

Henry presently discovered that, to stay in the village a looker-on while the love affair of Madeline and Cordis progressed to its consummation, was going to be too much for him. Instead of his getting used to the situation, it seemed to grow daily more insufferable. Every evening the thought that they were together made him feverish and restless till toward midnight, when, with the reflection that Cordis had surely by that time left her, came a possibility of sleep.

And yet, all this time he was not conscious of any special hate toward that young man.. If he had been in his power he would probably have left him unharmed. He could not, indeed, have raised his hand against anything which Madeline cared for. However great his animosity had been, that fact would have made his rival taboo to him. That Madeline had turned away from him was the great matter. Whither she was turned was of subordinate importance. His trouble was that she loved Cordis, not that Cordis loved her. It is only low and narrow natures which can find vent for their love disappointments in rage against their successors. In the strictest, truest sense, indeed, although it is certainly a hard saying, there is no room in a clear mind for such a feeling of jealousy. For the way in which every two hearts approach each other is necessarily a peculiar combination of individualities, never before and never after exactly duplicated in human experience. So that, if we can conceive of a woman truly loving several lovers, whether successively or simultaneously, they would not be rivals, for the manner of her love for each, and the manner of each one's love for her, is peculiar and single, even as if they two were alone in the world. The higher the mental grade of the persons concerned, the wider their sympathies, and the more delicate their perceptions, the more true is this.

Henry had been recently offered a very good position in an arms manufactory in Boston, and, having made up his mind to leave the village, he wrote to accept it, and promptly followed his letter, having first pledged his sole Newville correspondent, Laura, to make no references to Madeline in her letters.

"If they should be married," he was particular to say, "don't tell me about it till some time afterward."

Perhaps he worked the better in his new place because he was unhappy. The foe of good work is too easy self-complacency, too ready self-satisfaction, and the tendency to a pleased and relaxed contemplation of life and one's surroundings, growing out of a well-to-do state. Such a smarting sense of defeat, of endless aching loss as filled his mind at this time, was a most exacting background for his daily achievements in business and money-making to show up against. He had lost that power of enjoying rest which is at once the reward and limitation of human endeavour. Work was his nepenthe, and the difference between poor, superficial work and the best, most absorbing, was simply that between a weaker and a stronger opiate. He prospered in his affairs, was promoted to a position of responsibility with a good salary, and, moreover, was able to dispose of a patent in gun-barrels at a handsome price.

With the hope of distracting his mind from morbid brooding over what was past helping, he went into society, and endeavoured to interest himself in young ladies. But in these efforts his success was indifferent. Whenever he began to flatter himself that he was gaining a philosophical calm, the glimpse of some face on the street that reminded him of Madeline's, an accent of a voice that recalled hers, the sight of her in a dream, brought back in a moment the old thrall and the old bitterness with undiminished strength.

Eight or nine months after he had left home the longing to return and see what had happened became irresistible. Perhaps, after all—

Although this faint glimmer of a doubt was of his own making, and existed only because he had forbidden Laura to tell him to the contrary, he actually took some comfort in it. While he did not dare to put the question to Laura, yet he allowed himself to dream that something might possibly have happened to break off the match. He was far, indeed, from formally consenting to entertain such a hope. He professed to himself that he had no doubt that she was married and lost to him for ever. Had anything happened to break off the match, Laura would certainly have lost no time in telling him such good news. It was childishness to fancy aught else. But no effort of the reason can quite close the windows of the heart against hope, and, like a furtive ray of sunshine finding its way through a closed shutter, the thought that, after all, she might be free surreptitiously illumined the dark place in which he sat.

When the train stopped at Newville he slipped through the crowd at the station with the briefest possible greetings to the acquaintances he saw, and set out to gain his father's house by a back street.

On the way he met Harry Tuttle, and could not avoid stopping to exchange a few words with him.. As they talked, he was in a miserable panic of apprehension lest Harry should blurt out something about Madeline's being married. He felt that he could only bear to hear it from Laura's lips. Whenever the other opened his mouth to speak, a cold dew started out on Henry's forehead for fear he was going to make some allusion to Madeline; and when at last they separated without his having done so, there was such weakness in his limbs as one feels who first walks after a sickness.

He saw his folly now, his madness, in allowing himself to dally with a baseless hope, which, while never daring to own its own existence, had yet so mingled its enervating poison with every vein that he had now no strength left to endure the disappointment so certain and so near. At the very gate of his father's house he paused. A powerful impulse seized him to fly. It was not yet too late. Why had he come? He would go back to Boston, and write Laura by the next mail, and adjure her to tell him nothing. Some time he might bear to hear the truth, but not to-day, not now; no, not now. What had he been thinking of to risk it? He would get away where nobody could reach him to slay with a word this shadow of a hope which had become such a necessity of life to him, as is opium to the victim whose strength it has sapped and alone replaces. It was too late! Laura, as she sat sewing by the window, had looked up and seen him, and now as he came slowly up the walk she appeared at the door, full of exclamations of surprise and pleasure. He went in, and they sat down.

"I thought I'd run out and see how you all were," he said, with a ghastly smile.

"I'm so glad you did! Father was wondering only this morning if you were never coming to see us again."

He wiped his forehead with his handkerchief.

"I thought I'd just run out and see you."

"Yes, I'm so glad you did!"

She did not show that she noticed his merely having said the same thing over.

"Are you pretty well this spring?" she asked.

"Yes, I'm pretty well."

"Father was so much pleased about your patent. He's ever so proud of you."

After a pause, during which Henry looked nervously from point to point about the room, he said—

"Is he?"

"Yes, very, and so am I."

There was a long silence, and Laura took up her work-basket, and bent her face over it, and seemed to have a good deal of trouble in finding some article in it.

Suddenly he said, in a quick, spasmodic way—

"Is Madeline married?"

Good God! Would she never speak!

56

"No," she answered, with a falling inflection.

His heart, which had stopped beating, sent a flood of blood through every artery. But she had spoken as if it were the worst of news, instead of good. Ah! could it be? In all his thoughts, in all his dreams by night or day, he had never thought, he had never dreamed of that.

"Is she dead?" he asked, slowly, with difficulty, his will stamping the shuddering thought into words, as the steel die stamps coins from strips of metal.

"No," she replied again, with the same ill-boding tone.

"In God's name, what is it?" he cried, springing to his feet. Laura looked out at the window so that she might not meet his eye as she answered, in a barely audible voice—

"There was a scandal, and he deserted her; and afterward—only last week—she ran away, nobody knows where, but they think to Boston."

It was about two o'clock in the afternoon when Henry heard the fate of Madeline. By four o'clock he was on his way back to Boston. The expression of his face as he sits in the car is not that which might be expected under the circumstances. It is not that of a man crushed by a hopeless calamity, but rather of one sorely stricken indeed, but still resolute, supported by some strong determination which is not without hope.

Before leaving Newville he called on Mrs. Brand, who still lived in the same house. His interview with her was very painful. The sight of him set her into vehement weeping, and it was long before he could get her to talk. In the injustice of her sorrow, she reproached him almost bitterly for not marrying Madeline, instead of going off and leaving her a victim to Cordis. It was rather hard for him to be reproached in this way, but he did not think of saying anything in self-justification. He was ready to take blame upon himself.' He remembered no more now how she had rejected, rebuffed, and dismissed him. He told himself that he had cruelly deserted her, and hung his head before the mother's reproaches.

57

The room in which they sat was the same in which he had waited that morning of the picnic, while in his presence she had put the finishing touches to her toilet. There, above the table, hung against the wall the selfsame mirror that on that morning had given back the picture of a girl in white, with crimson braid about her neck and wrists, and a red feather in the hat so jauntily perched above the low forehead— altogether a maiden exceedingly to be desired. Perhaps, somewhere, she was standing before a mirror at that moment. But what sort of a flush is it upon her cheeks? What sort of a look is it in her eyes? What is this fell shadow that has passed upon her face?

By the time Henry was ready to leave the poor mother had ceased her upbraidings, and had yielded quite to the sense of a sympathy, founded in a loss as great as her own, which his presence gave her. Re was the only one in all the world from whom she could have accepted sympathy, and in her lonely desolation it was very sweet. And at the last, when, as he was about to go, her grief burst forth afresh, he put his arm around her and drew her head to his shoulder, and tenderly soothed her, and stroked the thin grey hair, till at last the long, shuddering sobs grew a little calmer. It was natural that he should be the one to comfort her. It was his privilege. In the adoption of sorrow, and not of joy, he had taken this mother of his love to be his mother.

"Don't give her up," he said. "I will find her if she is alive."

CHAPTER **VII**

A search, continued unintermittingly for a week among the hotels and lodging-houses of Boston, proved finally successful. He found her. As she opened the door of the miserable apartment which she occupied, and saw who it was that had knocked, the hard, unbeautiful red of shame covered her face. She would have closed the door against him, had he not quickly stepped within. Her eyelids fluttered a moment, and then she met his gaze with a look of reckless hardihood. Still holding the door half open, she said—

"Henry Burr, what do you want?"

The masses of her dark hairs hung low about her neck in disorder, and even in that first glance his eye had noted a certain negligent untidiness about her toilet most different from her former ways. Her face was worn and strangely aged and saddened, but beautiful still with the quenchless beauty of the glorious eyes, though sleepless nights had left their dark traces round them;

"What do you want? Why do you come here?" she demanded again, in harsh, hard tones; for he had been too much moved in looking at her to reply at once.

Now, however, he took the door-handle out of her hand and closed the door, and said, with only the boundless tenderness of his moist eyes to mend the bluntness of the words—

"Madeline, I want you. I want you for my wife."

The faintest possible trace of scorn was perceptible about her lips, but her former expression of hard indifference was otherwise quite unchanged as she replied, in a spiritless voice—

"So you came here to mock me? It was taking a good deal of trouble, but it is fair you should have your revenge."

He came close up to her.

"I'm not mocking. I'm in earnest. I'm one of those fellows who can never love but one woman, and love her for ever and ever. If there were not a scrap of you left bigger than your thumb, I'd rather have it than any woman in the world."

And now her face changed. There came into it the wistful look of those before whom passes a vision of happiness not for them, a look such as might be in the face of a doomed spirit which, floating by, should catch a glimpse of heavenly meads, and be glad to have had it, although its own way lay toward perdition. With a sudden impulse she dropped upon her knee, and seizing the hem of his coat pressed it to her lips, and then, before he could catch her, sprang away, and stood with one arm extended toward him, the palm turned outward, warning him not to touch her. Her eyes were marvellously softened with the tears that suffused them, and she said—

"I thank you, Henry. You are very good. I did not think any man could be so good. Now I remember, you always were very good to me. It will make the laudanum taste much sweeter. No! no! don't! Pity my shame. Spare me that! Oh, don't!"

But he was stronger than she, and kissed her. It was the second time he had ever done it. Her eyes flashed angrily, but that was instantly past, and she fell upon a chair crying as if her heart would break, her hands dropping nervously by her sides; for this was that miserable, desolate sorrow which does not care to hide its flowing tears and wrung face.

"Oh, you might have spared me that! O God! was it not hard enough before?" she sobbed.

In his loving stupidity, thinking to reassure her, he had wounded the pride of shame, the last retreat of self-respect, that cruellest hurt of all. There was a long silence. She seemed to have forgotten that he was there. Looking down upon her as she sat desolate, degraded, hopeless before him, not caring to cover her face, his heart swelled till it seemed as if it would burst, with such a sense of piteous loyalty and sublimed devotion as a faithful subject in the brave old times might have felt towards his queen whom he has found in exile, rags, and penury. Deserted by gods and men she might be, but his queen for ever she was, whose feet he was honoured to kiss. But what a gulf between feeling this and making her understand his feeling!

At length, when her sobs had ceased, he said, quietly—

"Forgive me. I didn't mean to hurt your feelings."

"It's all the same. It's no matter," she answered, listlessly, wiping her eyes with her hand. "I wish you would go away, though, and leave me alone. What do you want with me?"

"I want what I have always wanted: I want you for my wife."

She looked at him with stupid amazement, as if the real meaning of this already once declared desire had only just distinctly reached her mind, or as if the effect of its first announcement had been quite effaced by the succeeding outburst.

"Why, I thought you knew! You can't have heard—about me," she said.

61

"I have heard, I know all," he exclaimed, taking a step forward and standing over her. "Forgive me, darling! forgive me for being almost glad when I heard that you were free, and not married out of my reach. I can't think of anything except that I've found you. It is you, isn't it? It is you. I don't care what's happened to you, if it is only you."

As he spoke in this vehement, fiery way, she had been regarding him with an expression of faint curiosity. "I believe you do really mean it," she said, wonderingly, lingering over the words; "you always were a queer fellow."

"Mean it!" he exclaimed, kneeling before her, his voice all tremulous with the hope which the slightly yielding intonation of her words had given him. "Yes—yes—I mean it."

The faint ghost of a smile, which only brought out the sadness of her face, as a taper in a crypt reveals its gloom, hovered about her eyes.

"Poor boy!" she said; "I've, treated you very badly. I was going to make an end of myself this afternoon, but I will wait till you are tired of your fancy for me. It will make but little difference. There! there! Please don't kiss me."

CHAPTER **VIII**

He did not insist on their marriage taking place at once, although in her mood of dull indifference she would not have objected to anything he might have proposed. It was his hope that after a while she might become calmer, and more cheerful. He hoped to take in his at the altar a hand a little less like that of a dead person.

Introducing her as his betrothed wife, he found her very pleasant lodgings with an excellent family, where he was acquainted, provided her with books and a piano, took her constantly out to places of amusement, and, in every way which his ingenuity could suggest, endeavoured to distract and divert her. To all this she offered neither objection nor suggestion, nor did she, beyond the usual conventional responses, show the slightest gratitude. It was as if she took it for granted that he understood, as she did, that all this was being done for himself, and not for her, she being quite past having anything done for her. Her only recognition of the reverential and considerate tenderness which he showed her was an occasional air of wonder that cut him to the quick. Shame, sorrow, and despair had incrusted her heart with a hard shell, impenetrable to genial emotions. Nor would all his love help him to get over the impression that she was no longer an acquaintance and familiar friend, but somehow a stranger.

So far as he could find out, she did absolutely nothing all day except to sit brooding. He could not discover that she so much as opened the books and magazines he sent her, and, to the best of his knowledge, she made little more use of her piano. His calls were sadly dreary affairs. He would ask perhaps half a dozen questions, which he had spent much care in framing with a view to interesting her. She would reply in monosyllables, with sometimes a constrained smile or two, and then, after sitting a while in silence, he would take his hat and bid her good-evening.

She always sat nowadays in an attitude which he had never seen her adopt in former times, her hands lying in her lap before her, and an absent expression on her face. As he looked at her sitting thus, and recalled her former vivacious self-assertion and ever-new caprices, he was overcome with the sadness of the contrast.

Whenever he asked her about her health, she replied that she was well; and, indeed, she had that appearance. Grief is slow to sap the basis of a healthy physical constitution. She retained all the contour of cheek and rounded fulness of figure which had first captivated his fancy in the days, as it seemed, so long ago.

He took her often to the theatre, because in the action of the play she seemed at times momentarily carried out of herself. Once, when they were coming home from a play, she called attention to some feature of it. It was the first independent remark she had made since he had brought her to her lodgings. In itself it was of no importance at all, but he was overcome with delight, as people are delighted with the first words that show returning interest in earthly matters on the part of a convalescing friend whose soul has long been hovering on the borders of death. It would sound laughable to explain how much he made of that little remark, how he spun it out, and turned it in and out, and returned to it for days afterward. But it remained isolated. She did not make another.

Nevertheless, her mind was not so entirely torpid as it appeared, nor was she so absolutely self-absorbed. One idea was rising day by day out of the dark confusion of her thoughts, and that was the goodness and generosity of her lover. In this appreciation there was not the faintest glows of gratitude. She left herself wholly out of the account as only one could do with whom wretchedness has abolished for the time all interest in self. She was personally past being benefited. Her sense of his love and generosity was as disinterested as if some other person had been their object. Her admiration was such as one feels for a hero of history or fiction.

Often, when all within her seemed growing hard and still and dead, she felt that crying would make her feel better. At such times, to help her to cry, for the tears did not flow easily, she would sit down to the piano, the only times she ever touched it, and play over some of the simple airs associated with her life at home. Sometimes, after playing and crying a while, she would lapse into sweetly mournful day-dreams of how happy she might have been if she had returned Henry's love in those old days. She wondered in a puzzled way why it was that she had not. It seemed so strange to her now that she could have failed in doing so. But all this time it was only as a might-have-been that she thought of loving him, as one who feels himself mortally sick thinks of what he might have done when he was well, as a life-convict thinks of what he might have done when free, as a disembodied spirit might think of what it might have done when living. The consciousness of her disgrace, ever with her, had, in the past month or two, built up an impassable wall between her past life and her present state of existence. She no longer thought of herself in the present tense, still less the future.

He had not kissed her since that kiss at their first interview, which threw her into such a paroxysm of weeping. But one evening, when she had been more silent and dull than usual, and more unresponsive to his efforts to interest her, as he rose to go he drew her a moment to his side and pressed his lips to hers, as if constrained to find some expression for the tenderness so cruelly balked of any outflow in words. He went quickly out, but she continued to stand motionless, in the attitude of one startled by a sudden discovery. There was a frightened look in her dilated eyes. Her face was flooded to the roots of her hair with a deep flush. It was a crimson most unlike the tint of blissful shame with which the cheeks announce love's dawn in happy hearts. She threw herself upon the sofa, and buried her scorched face in the pillow while her form shook with dry sobs.

Love had, in a moment, stripped the protecting cicatrice of a hard indifference from her smarting shame, and it was as if for the first time she were made fully conscious of the desperation of her condition.

The maiden who finds her stainless purity all too lustreless a gift for him she loves, may fancy what were the feelings of Madeline, as love, with its royal longing to give, was born in her heart. With what lilies of virgin innocence would she fain have rewarded her lover! but her lilies were yellow, their fragrance was stale. With what an unworn crown would she have crowned him! but she had rifled her maiden regalia to adorn an impostor. And love came to her now, not as to others, but whetting the fangs of remorse and blowing the fires of shame.

But one thing it opened her eyes to, and made certain from the first instant of her new consciousness, namely, that since she loved him she could not keep her promise to marry him. In her previous mood of dead indifference to all things, it had not mattered to her one way or the other. Reckless what became of her, she had only a feeling that seeing he had been so good he ought to have any satisfaction he could find in marrying her. But what her indifference would have abandoned to him her love could not endure the thought of giving. The worthlessness of the gift, which before had not concerned her, now made its giving impossible. While before she had thought with indifference of submitting to a love she did not return, now that she returned it the idea of being happy in it seemed to her guilty and shameless. Thus to gather the honey of happiness from her own abasement was a further degradation, compared with which she could now almost respect herself. The consciousness that she had taken pleasure in that kiss made her seem to herself a brazen thing.

Her heart ached with a helpless yearning over him for the disappointment she knew he must now suffer at her hands. She tried, but in vain, to feel that she might, after all, marry him, might do this crowning violence to her nature, and accept a shameful happiness for his sake.

One morning a bitter thing happened to her. She had slept unusually well, and her dreams had been sweet and serene, untinged by any shadow of her waking thoughts, as if, indeed, the visions intended for the sleeping brain of some fortunate woman had by mistake strayed into hers. For a while she had lain, half dozing, half awake, pleasantly conscious of the soft, warm bed, and only half emerged from the atmosphere of dreamland. As at last she opened her eyes, the newly risen sun, bright from his ocean bath, was shining into the room, and the birds were singing. A lilac bush before the window was moving in the breeze, and the shadows of its twigs were netting the sunbeams on the wall as they danced to and fro.

The spirit of the jocund morn quite carried her away, and all unthinkingly she bounded out into the room and, stood there with a smile of sheer delight upon her face. She had forgotten all about her shame and sorrow. For an instant they were as completely gone from her mind as if they had never been, and for that instant nowhere did the sun's far-reaching eye rest on a blither or more innocent face. Then memory laid its icy finger on her heart and stilled its bounding pulse. The glad smile went out, like a taper quenched in Acheron, and she fell prone upon the floor, crying with hard, dry sobs, "O God! O God! O God!"

That day, and for many days afterward, she thought again and again of that single happy instant ere memory reclaimed its victim. It was the first for so long a time, and it was so very sweet, like a drop of water to one in torment. What a heaven a life must be which had many such moments! Was it possible that once, long ago, her life had been such an one—that she could awake mornings and not be afraid of remembering? Had there ever been a time when the ravens of shame and remorse had not perched above her bed as she slept, waiting her waking to plunge their beaks afresh into her heart? That instant of happiness which had been given her, how full it had been of blithe thanks to God and sympathy with the beautiful life of the world! Surely it showed that she was not bad, that she could have such a moment. It showed her heart was pure; it was only her memory that was foul. It was in vain that she swept and washed all within, and was good, when all the while her memory, like a ditch from a distant morass, emptied its vile stream of recollections into her heart, poisoning all the issues of life.

Years before, in one of the periodical religious revivals at Newville, she had passed through the usual girlish experience of conversion. Now, indeed, was a time when the heavenly compensations to which religion invites the thoughts of the sorrowful might surely have been a source of dome relief. But a certain cruel clearness of vision, or so at least it seemed to her, made all reflections on this theme but an aggravation of her despair. Since the shadow had fallen on her life, with every day the sense of shame and grief had grown more insupportable. In proportion as her loathing of the sin had grown, her anguish on account of it had increased. It was a poison-tree which her tears watered and caused to shoot forth yet deeper roots, yet wider branches, overspreading her life with ever denser, more noxious shadows. Since, then, on earth the purification of repentance does but deepen the soul's anguish over the past, how should it be otherwise in heaven, all through eternity? The pure in heart that see God, thought the unhappy girl, must only be those that have always been so, for such as become pure by repentance and tears do but see their impurity plainer every day.

Her horror of such a heaven, where through eternity perfect purification should keep her shame undying, taught her unbelief, and turned her for comfort to that other deep instinct of humanity, which sees in death the promise of eternal sleep, rest, and oblivion. In these days she thought much of poor George Bayley, and his talk in the prayer-meeting the night before he killed himself. By the mystic kinship that had declared itself between their sorrowful destinies, she felt a sense of nearness to him greater than her new love had given or ever could give her toward Henry. She recalled how she had sat listening to George's talk that evening, pitifully, indeed, but only half comprehending what he meant, with no dim, foreboding warning that she was fated to reproduce his experience so closely. Yes, reproduce it, perhaps, God only knew, even to the end. She could not bear this always. She understood now—ah! how well—his longing for the river of Lethe whose waters give forgetfulness. She often saw his pale face in dreams, wearing the smile he wore as he lay in the coffin, a smile as if he had been washed in those waters he sighed for.

CHAPTER IX

Henry had not referred to their marriage after the first interview. From day to day, and week to week, he had put off doing so, hoping that she might grow into a more serene condition of mind. But in this respect the result had sadly failed to answer his expectation. He could not deny to himself that, instead of becoming more cheerful, she was relapsing into a more and more settled melancholy. From day to day he noted the change, like that of a gradual petrifaction, which went on in her face. It was as if before his eyes she were sinking into a fatal stupor, from which all his efforts could not rouse her.

There were moments when he experienced the chilling premonition of a disappointment, the possibility of which he still refused to actually entertain. He owned to himself that it was a harder task than he had thought to bring back to life one whose veins the frost of despair has chilled. There were, perhaps, some things too hard even for his love. It was doubly disheartening for him thus to lose confidence; not only on his own account, but on hers. Not only had he to ask himself what would become of his life in the event of failure, but what would become of hers? One day overcome by this sort of discouragement, feeling that he was not equal to the case, that matters were growing worse instead of better, and that he needed help from some source, he asked Madeline if he had not better write to her mother to come to Boston, so that they two could keep house together.

"No," she said in a quick, startled voice, looking up at him in a scared way.

He hastened to reassure her, and say that he had not seriously thought of it, but he noticed that during the rest of the evening she cast furtive glances of apprehension at him, as if suspicious that he had some plot against her. She had fled from home because she could not bear her mother's eyes.

Meanwhile he was becoming almost as preoccupied and gloomy as she, and their dreary interviews grew more dreary than ever, for she was now scarcely more silent than he. His constant and increasing anxiety, in addition to the duties of a responsible business position, began to tell on his health. The owner of the manufactory of which he was superintendent, called him into his office one day, and told him he was working too hard, and must take a little vacation. But he declined. Soon after a physician whom he knew buttonholed him on the street, and managed to get in some shrewd questions about his health. Henry owned he did not sleep much nights. The doctor said he must take a vacation, and, this being declared impossible, forced a box of sleeping powders on him, and made him promise to try them.

All this talk about his health; as well as his own sensations, set him to thinking of the desperate position in which Madeline would be left in the event of his serious sickness or death.

That very day he made up his mind that it would not do to postpone their marriage any longer. It seemed almost brutal to urge it on her in her present frame of mind, and yet it was clearly out of the question to protract the present situation.

The quarter of the city in which he resided was suburban, and he went home every night by the steam cars. As he sat in the car that evening waiting for the train to start, two gentlemen in the seat behind fell to conversing about a new book on mental physiology, embodying the latest discoveries. They kept up a brisk talk on this subject till Henry left the car. He could not, however, have repeated a single thing which they had said. Preoccupied with his own thoughts, he had only been dimly conscious what they were talking about. His ears had taken in their words, but he had heard as not hearing.

After tea, in the gloaming, he called, as usual, on Madeline. After a few casual words, he said, gently—

"Madeline, you remember you promised to marry me a few weeks ago. I have not hurried you, but I want you now. There is no use in waiting any longer, dear, and I want you."

She was sitting in a low chair, her hands folded in her lap, and as he spoke her head sank so low upon her breast that he could not see her face. He was silent for some moments waiting a reply, but she made none.

"I know it was only for my sake you promised," he said again. "I know it will be nothing to you, and yet I would not press you if I did not think I could make you happier so. I will give up my business for a time, and we will travel and see the world a little."

Still she did not speak, but it was to some extent a reassurance to him that she showed no agitation.

"Are you willing that we should be married in a few days?" he asked.

She lifted her head slowly, and looked at him steadfastly.

"You are right," she said. "It is useless to keep on this way any longer."

"You consent, then?" said he, quite encouraged by her quiet air and apparent willingness.

"Don't press me for an answer to-night," she replied, after a pause, during which she regarded him with a singular fixity of expression. "Wait till to-morrow. You shall have an answer to-morrow. You are quite right. I've been thinking so myself. It is no use to put it off any longer."

He spoke to her once or twice after this, but she was gazing out through the window into the darkening sky, and did not seem to hear him. He rose to go, and had already reached the hail, when she called him—

"Come back a moment Henry."

He came back.

"I want you to kiss me," she said.

She was standing in the middle of the room. Her tall figure in its black dress was flooded with the weird radiance of the rising moon, nor was the moonshine whiter than her cheek, nor sadder than her steadfast eyes. Her lips were soft and yielding, clinging, dewy wet. He had never thought a kiss could be so sweet, and yet he could have wept, he knew not why.

When he reached his lodgings he was in an extremely nervous condition. In spite of all that was painful and depressing in the associations of the event, the idea of having Madeline for his wife in a few days more had power to fill him with feverish excitement, an excitement all the more agitating because it was so composite in its elements, and had so little in common with the exhilaration and light-heartedness of successful lovers in general. He took one of the doctor's sleeping powders, tried to read a dry book oil electricity, endeavoured to write a business letter, smoked a cigar, and finally went to bed.

It seemed to him that he went all the next day in a dazed, dreaming state, until the moment when he presented himself, after tea, at Madeline's lodgings, and she opened the door to him. The surprise which he then experienced was calculated to arouse him had he been indeed dreaming. His first thought was that she had gone crazy, or else had been drinking wine to raise her spirits; for there was a flush of excitement on either cheek, and her eyes were bright and unsteady. In one hand she held, with a clasp that crumpled the leaves, a small scientific magazine, which he recognized as having been one of a bundle of periodicals that he had sent her. With her other hand, instead of taking the hand which he extended, she clutched his arm and almost pulled him inside the door.

"Henry, do you remember what George Bayley said that might in meeting, about the river of Lethe, in which, souls were bathed and forgot the past?"

"I remember something about it," he answered.

"There is such a river. It was not a fable. It has been found again," she cried.

"Come and sit down, dear don't excite yourself so much. We will talk quietly," he replied, with a pitiful effort to speak soothingly, for he made no question that her long brooding had affected her mind.

"Quietly! How do you suppose I can talk quietly?" she exclaimed excitedly, in her nervous irritation throwing off the hand which he had laid on her arm. "Henry, see here, I want to ask you something. Supposing anybody had done something bad and had been very sorry for it, and then had forgotten it all, forgotten it wholly, would you think that made them good again? Would it seem so to you? Tell me!"

"Yes, surely; but it isn't necessary they should forget, so long us they're sorry."

"But supposing they had forgotten too?"

"Yes, surely, it would be as if it had never been."

"Henry," she said, her voice dropping to a low, hushed tone of wonder, while her eyes were full of mingled awe and exultation, "what if I were to forget it, forget that you know, forget it all, everything, just as if it had never been?"

He stared at her with fascinated eyes. She was, indeed, beside herself. Grief had made her mad.. The significance of his expression seemed to recall her to herself, and she said—

"You don't understand. Of course not. You think I'm crazy. Here, take it. Go somewhere and read it. Don't stay here to do it. I couldn't stand to look on. Go! Hurry! Read it, and then come back."

She thrust the magazine into his hand, and almost pushed him out of the door. But he went no further than the hall. He could not think of leaving her in that condition. Then it occurred to him to look at the magazine. He opened it by the light of the hall lamp, and his eyes fell on these words, the title of an article: "The Extirpation of Thought Processes. A New Invention."

If she were crazy, here was at least the clue to her condition. He read on; his eyes leaped along the lines.

The writer began with a clear account of the discoveries of modern psychologists and physiologists as to the physical basis of the intellect, by which it has been ascertained that certain ones of the millions of nerve corpuscles or fibres in the grey substance in the brain, record certain classes of sensations and the ideas directly connected with them, other classes of sensations with the corresponding ideas being elsewhere recorded by other groups of corpuscles. These corpuscles of the grey matter, these mysterious and infinitesimal hieroglyphics, constitute the memory of the record of the life, so that when any particular fibre or group of fibres is destroyed certain memories or classes of memories are destroyed, without affecting others which are elsewhere embodied in other fibres. Of the many scientific and popular demonstrations of these facts which were adduced, reference was made to the generally known fact that the effect of disease or injury at certain points in the brain is to destroy definite classes of acquisitions or recollections, leaving others untouched. The article then went on to refer to the fact that one of the known effects of the galvanic battery as medically applied, is to destroy and dissolve morbid tissues, while leaving healthy ones unimpaired. Given then a patient, who by excessive indulgence of any particular train of thought, had brought the group of fibres which were the physical seat of such thoughts into a diseased condition, Dr. Gustav Heidenhoff had invented a mode of applying the galvanic battery so as to destroy the diseased corpuscles, and thus annihilate the class of morbid ideas involved beyond the possibility of recollection, and entirely without affecting other parts of the brain or other classes of ideas. The doctor saw patients Tuesdays and Saturdays at his office, 79 ——— Street.

Madeline was not crazy, thought Henry, as still standing under the hall lamp he closed the article, but Dr. Heidenhoff certainly was. Never had such a sad sense of the misery of her condition been borne in upon him, as when he reflected that it had been able to make such a farrago of nonsense seem actually creditable to her. Overcome with poignant sympathy, and in serious perplexity how best he could deal with her excited condition, he slipped out of the house and walked for an hour about the streets. Returning, he knocked again at the door of her parlour.

"Have you read it?" she asked, eagerly, as she opened it.

"Yes, I've read it. I did not mean to send you such trash. The man must be either an escaped lunatic or has tried his hand at a hoax. It is a tissue of absurdity."

He spoke bluntly, almost harshly, because he was in terror at the thought that she might be allowing herself to be deluded by this wild and baseless fancy, but he looked away as he spoke. He could not bear to see the effect of his words.

"It is not absurd," she cried, clasping his arm convulsively with both hands so that she hurt him, and looking fiercely at him out of hot, fevered eyes. "It is the most reasonable thing in the world. It must be true. There can be no mistake. God would not let me be so deceived. He is not so cruel. Don't tell me anything else."

She was in such a hysterical condition that he saw he must be very gentle.

"But, Madeline, you will admit that if he is not the greatest of all discoverers, he must be a dangerous quack. His process might kill you or make you insane. It must be very perilous."

"If I knew there were a hundred chances that it would kill me to one that it would succeed, do you think I would hesitate?" she cried.

The utmost concession that he could obtain her consent to was that he should first visit this Dr. Heidenhoff alone, and make some inquiries of and about him.

CHAPTER X

The next day he called at 79 —— Street. There was a modest shingle bearing the name "Dr. Gustav Heidenhoff" fastened up on the side of the house, which was in the middle of a brick block. On announcing that he wanted to see the doctor, he was ushered into a waiting-room, whose walls were hung with charts of the brain and nervous system, and presently a tall, scholarly-looking man, with a clean-shaven face, frosty hair, and very genial blue eyes, deep set beneath extremely bushy grey eyebrows, entered and announced himself as Dr. Heidenhoff. Henry, who could not help being very favourably impressed by his appearance, opened the conversation by saying that he wanted to make some inquiries about the Thought-extirpation process in behalf of a friend who was thinking of trying it. The doctor, who spoke English with idiomatic accuracy, though with a slightly German accent, expressed his willingness to give him all possible information, and answered all his questions with great apparent candour, illustrating his explanations by references to the charts which covered the walls of the office.

He took him into an inner office and showed his batteries, and explained that the peculiarity of his process consisted, not in any new general laws and facts of physiology which he had discovered, but entirely in peculiarities in his manner of applying his galvanic current, talking much about apodes, cathodes, catelectrotonus and anelectrotonus, resistance and rheostat, reactions, fluctuations, and other terms of galvano-therapeutics. The doctor frankly admitted that he was not in a way of making a great deal of money or reputation by his discovery. It promised too much, and people consequently thought it must be quackery, and as sufficient proof of this he mentioned that he had now been five years engaged in practising the Thought-extirpation process without having attained any considerable celebrity or attracting a great number of patients. But he had a sufficient support in other branches of medical practice, he added, and, so long as he had patients enough for experimentation with the aim of improving the process, he was quite satisfied.

He listened with great interest to Henry's account of Madeline's case. The success of galvanism in obliterating the obnoxious train of recollections in her case would depend, he said, on whether it had been indulged to an extent to bring about a morbid state of the brain fibres concerned. What might be conventionally or morally morbid or objectionable, was not, however, necessarily disease in the material sense, and nothing but experiment could absolutely determine whether the two conditions coincided in any case. At any rate, he positively assured Henry that no harm could ensue to the patient, whether the operation succeeded or not.

"It is a pity, young man," he said, with a flash of enthusiasm, "that you don't come to me twenty years later. Then I could guarantee your friend the complete extirpation of any class of inconvenient recollections she might desire removed, whether they were morbid or healthy; for since the great fact of the physical basis of the intellect has been established, I deem it only a question of time when science shall have so accurately located the various departments of thought and mastered the laws of their processes, that, whether by galvanism or some better process, the mental physician will be able to extract a specific recollection from the memory as readily as a dentist pulls a tooth, and as finally, so far as the prevention of any future twinges in that quarter are concerned. Macbeth's question, 'Canst thou not minister to a mind diseased; pluck from the memory a rooted sorrow; raze out the written troubles of the brain?' was a puzzler to the sixteenth century doctor, but he of the twentieth, yes, perhaps of the nineteenth, will be able to answer it affirmatively."

"Is the process at all painful ?"

"In no degree, my dear sir. Patients have described to me their sensations many times, and their testimony is quite in agreement. When the circuit is closed there is a bubbling, murmurous sound in the ears, a warm sensation where the wires touch the cranium, and a feeling as of a motion through the brain, entering at one point and going out at another. There are also sparks of fire seen under the closed eyelids, an unpleasant taste in the mouth, and a sensation of smell; that is all."

"But the mental sensations ?" said Henry. "I should think they must be very peculiar, the sense of forgetting in spite of one's self, for I suppose the patient's mind is fixed on the very thoughts which the intent of the operation is to extirpate."

"Peculiar? Oh no, not at all peculiar," replied the doctor. "There are abundant analogies for it in our daily experience. From the accounts of patients I infer that it is not different from one's sensations in falling asleep while thinking of something. You know that we find ourselves forgetting preceding links in the train of thought, and in turning back to recall what went before, what came after is meanwhile forgotten, the clue is lost, and we yield to a pleasing bewilderment which is presently itself forgotten in sleep. The next morning we may or may not recall the matter. The only difference is that after the deep sleep which always follows the application of my process we never recall it, that is, if the operation has been successful. It seems to involve no more interference with the continuity of the normal physical and mental functions than does an afternoon's nap."

"But the after-effects!" persisted Henry. "Patients must surely feel that they have forgotten something, even if they do not know what it is. They must feel that there is something gone out of their minds. I should think this sensation would leave them in a painfully bewildered state."

"There seems to be a feeling of slight confusion," said the doctor; "but it is not painful, not more pronounced, indeed, than that of persons who are trying to bring back a dream which they remember having had without being able to recall the first thing about what it was. Of course, the patient subsequently finds shreds and fragments of ideas, as well as facts in his external relations, which, having been connected with the extirpated subject, are now unaccountable. About these the feeling is, I suppose, like that of a man who, when he gets over a fit of drunkenness or somnambulism, finds himself unable to account for things which he has unconsciously said or done. The immediate effect of the operation, as I intimated before, is to leave the patient very drowsy, and the first desire is to sleep."

"Doctor," said Henry, "when you talk it all seems for the moment quite reasonable, but you will pardon me for saying that, as soon as you stop, the whole thing appears to be such an incredible piece of nonsense that I have to pinch myself to be sure I am not dreaming."

The doctor smiled.

"Well," said he, "I have been so long engaged in the practical application of the process that I confess I can't realize any element of the strange or mysterious about it. To the eye of the philosopher nothing is wonderful, or else you may say all things are equally so. The commonest and so-called simplest fact in the entire order of nature is precisely as marvellous and incomprehensible at bottom as the most uncommon and startling. You will pardon me if I say that it is only to the unscientific that it seems otherwise. But really, my dear sir, my process for the extirpation of thoughts was but the most obvious consequence of the discovery that different classes of sensations and ideas are localized in the brain, and are permanently identified with particular groups of corpuscles of the grey matter. As soon as that was known, the extirpating of special clusters of thoughts became merely a question of mechanical difficulties to be overcome, merely a nice problem in surgery, and not more complex than many which my brethren have solved in lithotomy and lithotrity, for instance."

"I suppose what makes the idea a little more startling," said Henry, "is the odd intermingling of moral and physical conceptions in the idea of curing pangs of conscience by a surgical operation."

"I should think that intermingling ought not to be very bewildering," replied the doctor, "since it is the usual rule. Why is it more curious to cure remorse by a physical act than to cause remorse by a physical act? And I believe such is the origin of most remorse."

"Yes," said Henry, still struggling to preserve his mental equilibrium against this general overturning of his prejudices. "Yes, but the mind consents to the act which causes the remorse, and I suppose that is what gives it a moral quality."

"Assuredly," replied the doctor; "and I take it for granted that patients don't generally come to me unless they have experienced very genuine and profound regret and sorrow for the act they wish to forget. They have already repented it, and, according to every theory of moral accountability, I believe it is held that repentance balances the moral accounts. My process, you see then, only completes physically what is already done morally. The ministers and moralists preach forgiveness and absolution on repentance, but the perennial fountain of the penitent's tears testifies how empty and vain such assurances are. I fulfil what they promise. They tell the penitent he is forgiven. I free him from his sin. Remorse and shame and wan regret have wielded their cruel sceptres over human lives from the beginning until now. Seated within the mysterious labyrinths of the brain, they have deemed their sway secure, but the lightning of science has reached them on their thrones and set their bondmen free;" and with an impressive gesture the doctor touched the battery at his side.

Without giving further details of his conversation with this strange Master of Life, it is sufficient to say that Henry finally agreed upon an appointment for Madeline on the following day, feeling something as if he were making an unholy compact with the devil. He could not possibly have said whether he really expected anything from it or not. His mind had been in a state of bewilderment and constant fluctuation during the entire interview, at one moment carried away by the contagious confidence of the doctor's tone, and impressed by his calm, clear, scientific explanations and the exhibition of the electrical apparatus, and the next moment reacting into utter scepticism and contemptuous impatience with himself for even listening to such a preposterous piece of imposition. By the time he had walked half a block, the sights and sounds of the busy street, with their practical and prosaic suggestions, had quite dissipated the lingering influence of the necromantic atmosphere of Dr. Heidenhoff's office, and he was sure that he had been a fool.

He went to see Madeline that evening, with his mind made up to avoid telling her, if possible, that he had made the appointment, and to make such a report as should induce her to dismiss the subject. But he found it was quite impossible to maintain any such reticence toward one in her excited and peremptory mood. He was forced to admit the fact of the appointment.

"Why didn't you make it in the forenoon?" she demanded.

"What for? It is only a difference of a few hours," he replied.

"And don't you think a few hours is anything to me?" she cried, bursting into hysterical tears.

"You must not be so confident," he expostulated. "It scares me to see you so when you are so likely to be disappointed. Even the doctor said he could not promise success. It would depend on many things."

"What is the use of telling me that ?" she said, suddenly becoming very calm. "When I've just one chance for life, do you think it is kind to remind me that it may fail? Let me alone to-night."

The mental agitation of the past two days, supervening on so long a period of profound depression, had thrown her into a state of agitation bordering on hysteria. She was constantly changing her attitude, rising and seating herself, and walking excitedly about. She would talk rapidly one moment, and then relapse into a sudden chilled silence in which she seemed to hear nothing. Once or twice she laughed a hard, unnatural laugh of pure nervousness.

Presently she said—

"After I've forgotten all about myself, and no longer remember any reason why I shouldn't marry you, you will still remember what I've forgotten, and perhaps you won't want me."

"You know very well that I want you any way, and just the same whatever happens or doesn't happen," he answered.

"I wonder whether it will be fair to let you marry me after I've forgotten," she continued, thoughtfully. "I don't know, but I ought to make you promise now that you won't ask me to be your wife, for, of course, I shouldn't then know any reason for refusing you."

"I wouldn't promise that."

"Oh, but you wouldn't do so mean a thing as to take an unfair advantage of my ignorance," she replied. "Any way, I now release you from your engagement to marry me, and leave you to do as you choose tomorrow after I've forgotten.

I would make you promise not to let me marry you then, if I did not feel that utter forgetfulness of the past will leave me as pure and as good as if—as if—I were like other women;" and she burst into tears, and cried bitterly for a while.

The completeness with which she had given herself up to the belief that on the morrow her memory was to be wiped clean of the sad past, alternately terrified him and momentarily seduced him to share the same fool's paradise of fancy. And it is needless to say that the thought of receiving his wife to his arms as fresh and virgin in heart and memory as when her girlish beauty first entranced him, was very sweet to his imagination.

"I suppose I'll have mother with me then," she said, musingly. "How strange it will be! I've been thinking about it all day. I shall often find her looking at me oddly, and ask her what she is thinking of, and she will put me off. Why, Henry, I feel as dying persons do about having people look at their faces after they are dead. I shouldn't like to have any of my enemies who knew all about me see me after I've forgotten. You'll take care that they don't, won't you, Henry?"

"Why, dear, that is morbid. What is it to a dead person, whose soul is in heaven, who looks at his dead face? It will be so with you after to-morrow if the process succeeds."

She thought a while, and then said, shaking her head—

"Well, anyhow, I'd rather none but my friends, of those who used to know me, should see me. You'll see to it, Henry. You may look at me all you please, and think of what you please as you look. I don't care to take away the memory of anything from you. I don't believe a woman ever trusted a man as I do you. I'm sure none ever had reason to. I should be sorry if you didn't know all my faults. If there's a record to be kept of them anywhere in the universe, I'd rather it should be in your heart than anywhere else, unless, maybe, God has a heart like yours;" and she smiled at him through those sweetest tears that ever well up in human eyes, the tears of a limitless and perfect trust.

At one o'clock the next afternoon Madeline was sitting on the sofa in Dr. Heidenhoff's reception-room with compressed lips and pale cheeks, while Henry was nervously striding to and fro across the room, and furtively watching her with anxious looks. Neither had had much to say that morning.

"All ready," said the doctor, putting his head in at the door of his office and again disappearing. Madeline instantly rose. Henry put his hand on her arm, and said—

"Remember, dear, this was your idea, not mine, and if the experiment fails that makes no difference to me." She bowed her head without replying, and they went into the office. Madeline, trembling and deadly pale, sat down in the operating chair, and her head was immovably secured by padded clamps. She closed her eyes and put her hand in Henry's.

"Now," said the doctor to her, "fix your attention on the class of memories which you wish destroyed; the electric current more readily follows the fibres which are being excited by the present passage of nervous force. Touch my arm when you find your thoughts somewhat concentrated."

In a few moments she pressed the doctor's arm, and instantly the murmurous, bubbling hum of the battery began. She, clasped Henry's hand a little firmer, but made no other sign. The noise stopped. The doctor was removing the clamps. She opened her eyes and closed them again drowsily.

"Oh, I'm so sleepy."

"You shall lie down and take a nap," said the doctor.

There was a little retiring-room connected with the office where there was a sofa. No sooner had she laid her head on the pillow than she fell asleep. The doctor and Henry remained in the operating office, the door into the retiring-room being just ajar, so that they could hear her when she awoke.

CHAPTER **XI**

"How long will she sleep, doctor?" asked Henry, after satisfying himself by looking through the crack of the door that she was actually asleep.

"Patients do not usually wake under an hour or two," replied the doctor. "She was very drowsy, and that is a good sign. I think we may have the best hopes of the result of the operation."

Henry walked restlessly to and fro. After Dr. Heidenhoff had regarded him a few moments, he said—

"You are nervous, sir. There is quite a time to wait, and it is better to remain as calm as possible, for, in the event of an unsatisfactory result, your friend will need soothing, and you will scarcely be equal to that if you are yourself excited. I have some very fair cigars here. Do me the honour to try one. I prescribe it medicinally. Your nerves need quieting;" and he extended his cigar-case to the young man.

As Henry with a nod of acknowledgment took a cigar and lit it, and resumed his striding to and fro, the doctor, who had seated himself comfortably, began to talk, apparently with the kindly intent of diverting the other's mind.

"There are a number of applications of the process I hope to make, which will be rather amusing experiments. Take, for instance, the case of a person who has committed a murder, come to me, and forgotten all about it. Suppose he is subsequently arrested, and the fact ascertained that while he undoubtedly committed the crime, he cannot possibly recall his guilt, and so far as his conscience is concerned, is as innocent as a new-born babe, what then? What do you think the authorities would do?"

"I think," said Henry, "that they would be very much puzzled what to do."

"Exactly," said the doctor; "I think so too. Such a case would bring out clearly the utter confusion and contradiction in which the current theories of ethics and moral responsibility are involved. It is time the world was waked up on that subject. I should hugely enjoy precipitating such a problem on the community. I'm hoping every day a murderer will come in and require my services.

"There is another sort of case which I should also like to have," he continued; shifting his cigar to the other side of his mouth, and uncrossing and recrossing his knees. "Suppose a man has dons another a great wrong, and, being troubled by remorse, comes to me and has the sponge of oblivion passed over that item in his memory. Suppose the man he has wronged, pursuing him with a heart full of vengeance, gets him at last in his power, but at the same time finds out that he has forgotten, and can't be made to remember, the act he desires to punish him for."

"It would be very vexatious," said Henry..

"Wouldn't it, though? I can imagine the pursuer, the avenger, if a really virulent fellow, actually weeping tears of despite as he stands before his victim and marks the utter unconsciousness of any offence with which his eyes meet his own. Such a look would blunt the very stiletto of a Corsican. What sweetness would there be in vengeance if the avenger, as he plunged the dagger in his victim's bosom, might not hiss in his ear, 'Remember!' As well find satisfaction in torturing an idiot or mutilating a corpse. I am not talking now of brutish fellows, who would kick a stock or stone which they stumbled over, but of men intelligent enough to understand what vengeance is."

"But don't you fancy the avenger, in the case you supposed, would retain some bitterness towards his enemy, even though he had forgotten the offence?"

"I fancy he would always feel a certain cold dislike and aversion for him," replied the doctor—"an aversion such as one has for an object or an animal associated with some painful experience; but any active animosity would be a moral impossibility, if he were quite certain that there was absolutely no guilty consciousness on the other's part.

"But scarcely any application of the process gives me so much pleasure to dream about as its use to make forgiving possible, full, free, perfect, joyous forgiving, in cases where otherwise, however good our intentions, it is impossible, simply because we cannot forget. Because they cannot forget, friends must part from friends who have wronged them, even though they do from their hearts wish them well. But they must leave them, for they cannot bear to look in their eyes and be reminded every time of some bitter thing. To all such what good tidings will it be to learn of my process!

"Why, when the world gets to understand about it I expect that two men or two women, or a man and a woman, will come in here, and say to me, 'We have quarrelled and outraged each other, we have injured our friend, our wife, our husband; we regret, we would forgive, but we cannot, because we remember. Put between us the atonement of forgetfulness, that we may love each other as of old,' and so joyous will be the tidings of forgiveness made easy and perfect, that none will be willing to waste even an hour in enmity. Raging foes in the heat of their first wrath will bethink themselves ere they smite, and come to me for a more perfect satisfaction of their feud than any vengeance could promise."

Henry suddenly stopped in his restless pacing, stepped on tiptoe to the slightly opened door of the retiring room, and peered anxiously in. He thought he heard a slight stir. But no; she was still sleeping deeply, her position quite unchanged. He drew noiselessly back, and again almost closed the door.

"I suppose," resumed the doctor, after a pause, "that I must prepare myself as soon as the process gets well enough known to attract attention to be roundly abused by the theologians and moralists. I mean, of course, the thicker-headed ones. They'll say I've got a machine for destroying conscience, and am sapping the foundations of society. I believe that is the phrase. The same class of people will maintain that it's wrong to cure the moral pain which results from a bad act who used to think it wrong to cure the physical diseases induced by vicious indulgence. But the outcry won't last long, for nobody will be long in seeing that the morality of the two kinds of cures is precisely the same, If one is wrong, the other is. If there is something holy and God-ordained in the painful consequences of sin, it is as wrong to meddle with those consequences when they are physical as when they are mental. The alleged reformatory effect of such suffering is as great in one case as the other. But, bless you, nobody nowadays holds that a doctor ought to refuse to set a leg which its owner broke when drunk or fighting, so that the man may limp through life as a warning to himself and others.

"I know some foggy-minded people hold in a vague way that the working of moral retribution is somehow more intelligent, just, and equitable than the working of physical retribution. They have a nebulous notion that the law of moral retribution is in some peculiar way God's law, while the law of physical retribution is the law of what they call nature, somehow not quite so much God's law as the other is. Such an absurdity only requires to be stated to be exposed. The law of moral retribution is precisely as blind, deaf, and meaningless, and entitled to be respected just as little, as the law of physical retribution. Why, sir, of the two, the much-abused law of physical retribution is decidedly more moral, in the sense of obvious fairness, than the so-called law of moral retribution itself. For, while the hardened offender virtually escapes all pangs of conscience, he can't escape the diseases and accidents which attend vice and violence. The whole working of moral retribution, on the contrary, is to torture the sensitive-souled, who would never do much harm any way, while the really hard cases of society, by their very hardness, avoid all suffering. And then, again, see how merciful and reformatory is the working of physical retribution compared with the pitilessness of the moral retribution of memory. A man gets over his accident or disease and is healthy again, having learned his lesson with the renewed health that alone makes it of any value to have had that lesson. But shame and sorrow for sin and disgrace go on for ever increasing in intensity, in proportion as they purify the soul. Their worm dieth not, and their fire is not quenched. The deeper the repentance, the more intense the longing and love for better things, the more poignant the pang of regret and the sense of irreparable loss. There is no sense, no end, no use, in this law which increases the severity of the punishment as the victim grows in innocency.

"Ah, sir," exclaimed the doctor, rising and laying his hand caressingly on the battery, while a triumphant exultation shone in his eyes, "you have no idea of the glorious satisfaction I take in crushing, destroying, annihilating these black devils of evil memories that feed on hearts. It is a triumph like a god's.

"But oh, the pity of it, the pity of it!" he added, sadly, as his hand fell by his side, "that this so simple discovery has come so late in the world's history! Think of the infinite multitude of lives it would have redeemed from the desperation of hopelessness, or the lifelong shadow of paralysing grief to all manner of sweet, good, and joyous uses!"

Henry opened the door slightly, and looked into the retiring-room. Madeline was lying perfectly motionless, as he had seen her before. She had not apparently moved a muscle. With a sudden fear at his heart, he softly entered, and on tiptoe crossed the room and stood over her. The momentary fear was baseless. Her bosom rose and fell with long, full breathing, the faint flush of healthy sleep tinged her cheek, and the lips were relaxed in a smile. It was impossible not to feel, seeing her slumbering so peacefully, that the marvellous change had been indeed wrought, and the cruel demons of memory that had so often lurked behind the low, white forehead were at last no more.

When he returned to the office, Dr. Heidenhoff had seated himself, and was contemplatively smoking.

"She was sleeping, I presume," he said.

"Soundly," replied Henry.

"That is well. I have the best of hopes. She is young. That is a favourable element in an operation of this sort."

Henry said nothing, and there was a considerable silence. Finally the doctor observed, with the air of a man who thinks it just as well to spend the time talking—

"I am fond of speculating what sort of a world, morally speaking, we should have if there were no memory. One thing is clear, we should have no such very wicked people as we have now. There would, of course, be congenitally good and bad dispositions, but a bad disposition would not grow worse and worse as it does now, and without this progressive badness the depths of depravity are never attained."

"Why do you think that?"

"Because it is the memory of our past sins which demoralizes as, by imparting a sense of weakness and causing loss of self-respect. Take the memory away, and a bad act would leave us no worse in character than we were before its commission, and not a whit more likely to repeat it than we were to commit it the first time."

"But surely our good or bad acts impress our own characters for good or evil, and give an increased tendency one way or the other."

"Excuse me, my dear sir. Acts merely express the character. The recollection of those acts is what impresses the character, and gives it a tendency in a particular direction. And that is why I say, if memory were abolished, constitutionally bad people would remain at their original and normal degree of badness, instead of going from bad to worse, as they always have done hitherto in the history of mankind. Memory is the principle of moral degeneration. Remembered sin is the most utterly diabolical influence in the universe. It invariably either debauches or martyrizes men and women, accordingly as it renders them desperate and hardened, or makes them a prey to undying grief and self-contempt. When I consider that more sin is the only anodyne for sin, and that the only way to cure the ache of conscience is to harden it, I marvel that even so many as do essay the bitter and hopeless way of repentance and reform. In the main, the pangs of conscience, so much vaunted by some, do most certainly drive ten deeper into sin where they bring one back to virtue."

"But," remarked Henry, "suppose there were no memory, and men did forget their acts, they would remain just as responsible for them as now."

"Precisely; that is, not at all," replied the doctor.

"You don't mean to say there is no such thing as responsibility, no such thing as justice. Oh, I see, you deny free will. You are a necessitarian."

The doctor waved his hand rather contemptuously.

"I know nothing about your theological distinctions; I am a doctor. I say that there is no such thing as moral responsibility for past acts, no such thing as real justice in punishing them, for the reason that human beings are not stationary existences, but changing, growing, incessantly progressive organisms, which in no two moments are the same. Therefore justice, whose only possible mode of proceeding is to punish in present time for what is done in past time, must always punish a person more or less similar to, but never identical with, the one who committed the offence, and therein must be no justice.

"Why, sir, it is no theory of mine, but the testimony of universal consciousness, if you interrogate it aright, that the difference between the past and present selves of the same individual is so great as to make them different persons for all moral purposes. That single fact we were just speaking of—the fact that no man would care for vengeance on one who had injured him, provided he knew that all memory of the offence had been blotted utterly from his enemy's mind—proves the entire proposition. It shows that it is not the present self of his enemy that the avenger is angry with at all, but the past self. Even in the blindness of his wrath he intuitively recognizes the distinction between the two. He only hates the present man, and seeks vengeance on him in so far as he thinks that he exults in remembering the injury his past self did, or, if he does not exult, that he insults and humiliates him by the bare fact of remembering it. That is the continuing offence which alone keeps alive the avenger's wrath against him. His fault is not that he did the injury, for _he_ did not do it, but that he remembers it.

"It is the first principle of justice, isn't it, that nobody ought to be punished for what he can't help? Can the man of to-day prevent or affect what he did yesterday, let me say, rather, what the man did out of whom he has grown—has grown, I repeat, by a physical process which he could not check save by suicide. As well punish him for Adam's sin, for he might as easily have prevented that, and is every whit as accountable for it. You pity the child born, without his choice, of depraved parents. Pity the man himself, the man of today who, by a process as inevitable as the child's birth, has grown on the rotten stock of yesterday. Think you, that it is not sometimes with a sense of loathing and horror unutterable, that he feels his fresh life thus inexorably knitting itself on, growing on, to that old stem? For, mind you well, the consciousness of the man exists alone in the present day and moment. There alone he lives. That is himself. The former days are his dead, for whose sins, in which he had no part, which perchance by his choice never would have been done, he is held to answer and do penance. And you thought, young man, that there was such a thing as justice !"

"I can see," said Henry, after a pause, "that when half a lifetime has intervened between a crime and its punishment, and the man has reformed, there is a certain lack of identity. I have always thought punishments in such cases very barbarous. I know that I should think it hard to answer for what I may have done as a boy, twenty years ago.

"Yes," said the doctor, "flagrant cases of that sort take the general eye, and people say that they are instances of retribution rather than justice. The unlikeness between the extremes of life, as between the babe and the man, the lad and the dotard, strikes every mind, and all admit that there is not any apparent identity between these widely parted points in the progress of a human organism. How then? How soon does identity begin to decay, and when is it gone—in one year, five years, ten years, twenty years, or how many? Shall we fix fifty years as the period of a moral statute of limitation, after which punishment shall be deemed barbarous? No, no. The gulf between the man of this instant and the man of the last is just as impassable as that between the baby and the man. What is past is eternally past. So far as the essence of justice is concerned, there is no difference between one of the cases of punishment which you called barbarous, and one in which the penalty follows the offence within the hour. There is no way of joining the past with the present, and there is no difference between what is a moment past and what is eternally past."

"Then the assassin as he withdraws the stiletto from his victim's breast is not the same man who plunged it in."

"Obviously not," replied the doctor. "He may be exulting in the deed, or, more likely, he may be in a reaction of regret. He may be worse, he may be better. His being better or worse makes it neither more nor less just to punish him, though it may make it more or less expedient. Justice demands identity; similarity, however close, will not answer. Though a mother could not tell her twin sons apart, it would not make it any more just to punish one for the other's sins."

"Then you don't believe in the punishment of crime?" said Henry.

"Most emphatically I do," replied the doctor; "only I don't believe in calling it justice or ascribing it a moral significance. The punishment of criminals is a matter of public policy and expediency, precisely like measures for the suppression of nuisances or the prevention of epidemics. It is needful to restrain those who by crime have revealed their likelihood to commit further crimes, and to furnish by their punishment a motive to deter others from crime."

"And to deter the criminal himself after his release," added Henry.

"I included him in the word 'others,'" said the doctor. "The man who is punished is other from the man who did the act, and after punishment he is still other."

"Really, doctor," observed Henry, "I don't see that a man who fully believes your theory is in any need of your process for obliterating his sins. He won't think of blaming himself for them any way."

"True," said the doctor, "perfectly true. My process is for those who cannot attain to my philosophy. I break for the weak the chain of memory which holds them to the past; but stronger souls are independent of me. They can unloose the iron links and free themselves. Would that more had the needful wisdom and strength thus serenely to put their past behind them, leaving the dead to bury their dead, and go blithely forward, taking each new day as a life by itself, and reckoning themselves daily new-born, even as verily they are! Physically, mentally, indeed, the present must be for ever the outgrowth of the past, conform to its conditions, bear its burdens; but moral responsibility for the past the present has none, and by the very definition of the words can have none. There is no need to tell people that they ought to regret and grieve over the errors of the past. They can't help doing that. I myself suffer at times pretty sharply from twinges of the rheumatism which I owe to youthful dissipation. It would be absurd enough for me, a quiet old fellow of sixty, to take blame to myself for what the wild student did, but, all the same, I confoundedly wish he hadn't.

"Ah, me!" continued the doctor. "Is there not sorrow and wrong enough in the present world without having moralists teach us that it is our duty to perpetuate all our past sins and shames in the multiplying mirror of memory, as if, forsooth, we were any more the causers of the sins of our past selves than of our fathers' sins. How many a man and woman have poisoned their lives with tears for some one sin far away in the past! Their folly is greater, because sadder, but otherwise just like that of one who should devote his life to a mood of fatuous and imbecile self-complacency over the recollection of a good act he had once done. The consequences of the good and the bad deeds our fathers and we have done fall on our heads in showers, now refreshing, now scorching, of rewards and of penalties alike undeserved by our present selves. But, while we bear them with such equanimity as we may, let us remember that as it is only fools who flatter themselves on their past virtues, so it is only a sadder sort of fools who plague themselves for their past faults."

Henry's quick ear caught a rustle in the retiring-room. He stepped to the door and looked in. Madeline was sitting up.

CHAPTER **XII**

Her attitude was peculiar. Her feet were on the floor, her left hand rested on the sofa by her side, her right was raised to one temple and checked in the very act of pushing back a heavy braid of hair which had been disarranged in sleep. Her eyebrows were slightly contracted, and she was staring at the carpet. So concentrated did her faculties appear to be in the effort of reflection that she did not notice Henry's entrance until, standing by her aide, he asked, in a voice which he vainly tried to steady—

"How do you feel ?"

She did not look up at him at all, but replied, in the dreamy, drawling tone of one in a brown study—

"I—feel—well. I'm—ever—so—rested."

"Did you just wake up?" he said, after a moment. He did not know what to say.

She now glanced up at him, but with an expression of only partial attention, as if still retaining a hold on the clue of her thoughts.

"I've been awake some time trying to think it out," she said.

"Think out what?" he asked, with a feeble affectation of ignorance. He was entirely at loss what course to take with her.

"Why, what it was that we came here to have me forget," she said, sharply. "You needn't think the doctor made quite a fool of me. It was something like hewing, harring, Howard. It was something that began with 'H,' I'm quite sure. 'H,'" she continued, thoughtfully, pressing her hand on the braid she was yet in the act of pushing back from her forehead. "'H,'— or maybe—'K.' Tell me, Henry. You must know, of course."

"Why—why," he stammered in consternation. "If you came here to forget it, what's the use of telling you, now you've forgotten it, that is—I mean, supposing there was anything to forget."

"I haven't forgotten it," she declared. "The process has been a failure anyhow. It's just puzzled me for a minute. You might as well tell me. Why, I've almost got it now. I shall remember it in a minute," and she looked up at him as if she were on the point of being vexed with his obstinacy. The doctor coming into the room at this moment, Henry turned to him in his perplexity, and said—

"Doctor, she wants to know what it was you tried to make her forget."

"What would you say if I told you it was an old love affair?" replied the doctor, coolly.

"I should say that you were rather impertinent," answered Madeline, looking at him somewhat haughtily.

"I beg your pardon. I beg your pardon, my dear. You do well to resent it, but I trust you will not be vexed with an old gentleman," replied the doctor, beaming on her from under his bushy eyebrows with an expression of gloating benevolence.

99

"I suppose, doctor, you were only trying to plague me so as to confuse me," she said, smiling. "But you can't do it. I shall remember presently. It began with 'H'—I am almost sure of that. Let's see—Harrington, Harvard. That's like it."

"Harrison Cordis, perhaps," suggested the doctor, gravely.

"Harrison Cordis? Harrison? Harrison?" she repeated, contracting her eyebrows thoughtfully; "no, it was more like Harvard. I don't want any more of your suggestions. You'd like to get me off the track."

The doctor left the room, laughing, and Henry said to her, his heart swelling with an exultation which made his voice husky, "Come, dear, we had better go now: the train leaves at four."

"I'll remember yet," she said, smiling at him with a saucy toss of the head. He put out his arms and she came into them, and their lips met in a kiss, happy and loving on her part, and fraught with no special feeling, but the lips which hers touched were tremulous. Slightly surprised at his agitation, she leaned back in his clasp, and, resting her glorious black eyes on his, said—

"How you love me, dear!"

Oh, the bright, sweet light in her eyes! the light he had not seen since she was a girl, and which had never shone for him before. As they were about to leave, the doctor drew him aside.

"The most successful operation I ever made, sir," he said, enthusiastically. "I saw you were startled that I should tell her so frankly what she had forgotten. You need not have been so. That memory is absolutely gone, and cannot be restored. She might conclude that what she had forgotten was anything else in the world except what if really was. You may always allude with perfect safety before her to the real facts, the only risk being that, if she doesn't think you are making a bad joke, she will be afraid that you are losing your mind."

All the way home Madeline was full of guesses and speculation as to what it had been which she had forgotten, finally, however, settling down to the conclusion that it had something to do with Harvard College, and when Henry refused to deny explicitly that such was the case, she was quite sure. She announced that she was going to get a lot of old catalogues and read over the names, and also visit the college to see if she could not revive the recollection. But, upon his solemnly urging her not to do so, lest she might find her associations with that institution not altogether agreeable if revived, she consented to give up the plan.

"Although, do you know," she said, "there is nothing in the world which I should like to find out so much as what it was we went to Dr. Heidenhoff in order to make me forget. What do you look so sober for? Wouldn't I really be glad if I could?"

"It's really nothing of any consequence," he said, pretending to be momentarily absorbed in opening his penknife.

"Supposing it isn't, it's just as vexatious not to remember it," she declared.

"How did you like Dr. Heidenhoff?" he asked.

"Oh, I presume he's a good enough doctor, but I thought that joke about an affair of the heart wasn't at all nice. Men are so coarse."

"Oh, he meant no harm," said Henry, hastily.

"I suppose he just tried to say the absurdest thing he could think of to put me off the track and make me laugh. I'm sure I felt more like boxing his ears. I saw you didn't like it either, sir."

"How so?"

"Oh, you needn't think I didn't notice the start you gave when he spoke, and the angry way you looked at him. You may pretend all you want to, but you can't cheat me. You'd be the very one to make an absurd fuss if you thought I had even so much as looked at anybody else." And then she burst out laughing at the red and pale confusion of his face. "Why, you're the very picture of jealousy at the very mention of the thing. Dear me, what a tyrant you are going to be! I was going to confess a lot of my old flirtations to you, but now I sha'n't dare to. O Henry, how funny my face feels when I laugh, so stiff, as if the muscles were all rusty! I should think I hadn't laughed for a year by the feeling."

He scarcely dared leave her when they reached her lodgings, for fear that she might get to thinking and puzzling over the matter, and, possibly, at length might hit upon a clue which, followed up, would lead her back to the grave so recently covered over in her life, and turn her raving mad with the horror of the discovery. As soon as he possibly could, he almost ran back to her lodgings in a panic. She had evidently been thinking matters over.

"How came we here in Boston together, Henry? I don't seem to quite understand why I came. I remember you came after me?"

"Yes, I came after you."

"What was the matter? Was I sick?"

"Very sick."

"Out of my head?"

"Yes."

"That's the reason you took me to the doctor, I suppose?"

"Yes."

"But why isn't mother here with me?"

"You—you didn't seem to want her," answered Henry, a cold sweat covering his face under this terrible inquisition.

"Yes," said she, slowly, "I do remember your proposing she should come and my not wanting her. I can't imagine why. I must have been out of my head, as you say. Henry," she continued, regarding him with eyes of sudden softness, "you must have been very good to me. Dr. Heidenhoff could never make me forget that."

The next day her mother came. Henry met her at the station and explained everything to her, so that she met Madeline already prepared for the transformation, that is, as much prepared as the poor woman could be. The idea was evidently more than she could take in. In the days that followed she went about with a dazed expression on her face, and said very little. When she looked at Henry, it was with a piteous mingling of gratitude and appeal. She appeared to regard Madeline with a bewilderment that increased rather than decreased from day to day. Instead of becoming familiar with the transformation, the wonder of it evidently grew on her. The girl's old, buoyant spirits, which had returned in full flow, seemed to shock and pain her mother with a sense of incongruity she could not get over. When Madeline treated her lover to an exhibition of her old imperious tyrannical ways, which to see again was to him sweeter than the return of day, her mother appeared frightened, and would try feebly to check her, and address little deprecating remarks to Henry that were very sad to hear. One evening, when he came in in the twilight, he saw Madeline sitting with "her baby," as she had again taken to calling her mother, in her arms, rocking and soothing her, while the old lady was drying and sobbing on her daughter's bosom.

"She mopes, poor little mother!" said Madeline to Henry. "I can't think what's the matter with her. We'll take her off with us on our wedding trip. She needs a little change."

"Dear me, no, that will never do," protested the little woman, with her usual half-frightened look at Henry. "Mr. Burr wouldn't think that nice at all."

"I mean that Mr. Burr shall be too much occupied in thinking how nice I am to do any other thinking," said Madeline.

"That's like the dress you wore to the picnic at Hemlock Hollow," said Henry.

"Why, no, it isn't either. It only looks a little like it. It's light, and cut the same way; that's all the resemblance; but of course a man couldn't be expected to know any better."

103

"It's exactly like it," maintained Henry.

"What'll you bet?"

"I'll bet the prettiest pair of bracelets I can find in the city."

"Betting is wicked," said Madeline, "and so I suppose it's my duty to take this bet just to discourage you from betting any more. Being engaged makes a girl responsible for a young man's moral culture."

She left the room, and returned in a few moments with the veritable picnic dress on.

"There!" she said, as she stepped before the mirror.

"Ah, that's it, that's it! I give in," he exclaimed, regarding her ecstatically. "How pretty you were that day! I'd never seen you so pretty before. Do you remember that was the day I kissed you first? I should never have dared to. I just had to—I couldn't help it."

"So I believe you said at the time," observed Madeline, dryly. "It does make me not so bad," she admitted, inspecting herself with a critical air. "I really don't believe you could help it. I ought not to have been so hard on you, poor boy. There! there! I didn't mean that. Don't! Here comes mother."

Mrs. Brand entered the room, bringing a huge pasteboard box.

"Oh, she's got my wedding dress! Haven't you, mother?" exclaimed Madeline, pouncing on the box. "Henry, you might as well go right home. I can't pay any more attention to you to-night. There's more important business."

"But I want to see you with it on," he demurred.

"You do?"

"Yes."

"Very much?"

"The worst kind."

"Well, then, you sit down and wait here by yourself for about an hour, and maybe you shall;" and the women were off upstairs.

At length there was a rustling on the stairway, and she re-entered the room, all sheeny white in lustrous satin. Behind the gauzy veil that fell from the coronal of dark brown hair adown the shoulders her face shone with a look he had never seen in it. It was no longer the mirthful, self-reliant girl who stood before him, but the shrinking, trustful bride. The flashing, imperious expression that so well became her bold beauty at other times had given place to a shy and blushing softness, inexpressibly charming to her lover. In her shining eyes a host of virginal alarms were mingled with the tender, solemn trust of love.

As he gazed, his eyes began to swim with tenderness, and her face grew dim and misty to his vision. Then her white dress lost its sheen and form, and he found himself staring at the white window-shade of his bedroom, through which the morning light was peering. Startled, bewildered, he raised himself on his elbow in bed. Yes, he was in bed. He looked around, mechanically taking note of one and another familiar feature of the apartment to make sure of his condition. There, on the stand by his bedside, lay his open watch, still ticking, and indicating his customary hour of rising. There, turned on its face, lay that dry book on electricity he had been reading himself to sleep with. And there, on the bureau, was the white paper that had contained the morphine sleeping powder which he took before going to bed. That was what had made him dream. For some of it must have been a dream! But how much of it was a dream? Re must think. That was a dream certainly about her wedding dress. Yes, and perhaps—yes, surely—that must be a dream about her mother's being in Boston. He could not remember writing Mrs. Brand since Madeline had been to Dr. Heidenhoff. He put his hand to his forehead, then raised his head and looked around the room with an appealing stare. Great God! why, that was a dream too! The last waves of sleep ebbed from his brain and to his aroused consciousness the clear, hard lines of reality dissevered themselves sharply from the vague contours of dreamland. Yes, it was all a dream. He remembered how it all was now. He had not seen Madeline since the evening before, when he had proposed their speedy marriage, and she had called him back in that strange way to kiss her. What a dream! That sleeping powder had done it—that, and the book on electricity, and that talk on mental physiology which he had overheard in the car the afternoon before. These rude materials, as unpromising as the shapeless bits of glass which the kaleidoscope turns into schemes of symmetrical beauty, were the stuff his dream was made of.

It was a strange dream indeed, such an one as a man has once or twice in a lifetime. As he tried to recall it, already it was fading from his remembrance. That kiss Madeline had called him back to give him the night before; that had been strange enough to have been a part also of the dream. What sweetness, what sadness, were in the touch of her lips. Ah! when she was once his wife, he could contend at better advantage with her depression of spirits, He would hasten their marriage. If possible, it should take place that very week.

There was a knock at the door. The house-boy entered, gave him a note, and went out. It was in Madeline's hand, and dated the preceding evening. It read as follows:—

"You have but just gone away. I was afraid when I kissed you that you would guess what I was going to do, and make a scene about it, and oh, dear! I am so tired that I couldn't bear a scene. But you didn't think. You took the kiss for a promise of what I was to be to you, when it only meant what I might have been. Poor, dear boy! it was just a little stupid of you not to guess. Did you suppose I would really marry you? Did you really think I would let you pick up from the gutter a soiled rose to put in your bosom when all the fields are full of fresh daisies? Oh, I love you too well for that! Yes, dear, I love you. I've kept the secret pretty well, haven't I? You see, loving you has made me more careful of your honour than when in my first recklessness I said I would marry you in spite of all. But don't think, dear, because I love you that it is a sacrifice I make in not being your wife. I do truly love you, but I could not be happy with you, for my happiness would be shame to the end. It would be always with us as in the dismal weeks that now are over. The way I love you is not the way I loved him, but it is a better way. I thought perhaps you would like to know that you alone have any right to kiss my lips in dreams. I speak plainly of things we never spoke of, for you know people talk freely when night hides their faces from each other, and how much more if they know that no morning shall ever come to make them shamefaced again! A certain cold white hand will have wiped away the flush of shame for ever from my face when you look on it again, for I go this night to that elder and greater redeemer whose name is death. Don't blame me, dear, and say I was not called away. Is it only when death touches our bodies that we are called? Oh, I am called, I am called, indeed!

"MADELINE."

www.ingramcontent.com/pod-product-compliance
Lightning Source LLC
Chambersburg PA
CBHW020620130626
46552CB00003B/1056